The US Review of Books
Professional Reviews for the People

Wolfscape
by H. D. Duman
book review by Kellie Haulotte

"Blunt snout, canines gleaming with saliva, he surveyed the kill zone."

Frank and Alice Thompson take their first winter trip to the San Juan mountains, where their cabin is located. Things don't take long to turn terrible for them: their Chevy Blazer is dead and completely frozen, Alice forgets to pack the phone chargers, and they quickly run out of supplies. Frank decides that he will have to trek the twenty-two-mile hike to the town of Telluride, Colorado, or they won't survive. On the way, Frank is being stalked by an alpha wolf named Rollo. Rollo is changing into something beyond the usual wolf after a fight with a bear. The transformation is called the "splitting," and like Frank, Rollo is being hunted too. In the wolf's case, it is by his doppelganger. However, this entity or phantom has a purpose that's closer to Frank than imaginable. It's a battle between good and evil.

The story, both a psychological thriller and a classic adventure tale, is intertwined with elements of the supernatural. Duman's plot is fantastical to the very end. His main characters are well-written and rounded. This can be seen in the author's exploration of the Thompsons' relationship. Frank is a father, husband, and a tire salesman who seems to be on the edge. His and Alice's relationship is in a rut, which is one of the reasons why they decided to take the trip in the first place. However, Alice is worried about it because they are in their mid-forties and out of shape. Another high point in the story is the author's portrayal of the wolf's point of view. In fact, some of the best writing in the story is about Rollo and his inner thoughts. Overall, there is nothing ordinary about Duman's novel, which makes it all the better for readers.

ENDORSEMENT

I'd give Wolfscape six stars if I could! I hung on every descriptive word and event and couldn't wait to see what happened next, all while getting glimpses of the magnificent and beautiful Colorado Rocky Mountains. The ability to understand what each character was thinking, via the author's brilliant prose, brought common sense to each chilling situation. Until, I realized things don't happen that way in the real world, or do they?

~ Victor Kusske,
Author Criminal Prosecutor book series

The story takes place in Telluride, Colorado ringed by the majestic San Juan mountains. What a wonderful place to write a novel about two wolves, one evil and one good. The author wrote a very authentic and descriptive story that was most enjoyable. It's a must read.?

~ Carole Lorenz Thomas,
Oregon State University Alumnus and World Traveler.

WOLFSCAPE

ISBN: 978-1-965679-87-6 Paperback
ISBN: 978-1-965679-88-3 Ebook

Rev. date: 03/24/2025

WOLFSCAPE

H.D. Duman

CONTENTS

ACKNOWLEDGEMENT

I am indebted to Leavitt Peak Press for accepting my manuscript and publishing Wolfscape. I also give special thanks to my test readers for putting up with me. I deliberately blurred the lines, in some cases, between fact and fiction in order to give the story more impact. Any omissions and/or errors are, of course, all mine.

The characters in this book are entirely fictitious and any resemblance to persons living or dead is purely coincidental. Further, thanks to my sr. publicist, Lucy Lane who worked diligently to get Wolfscape published. Finally, to the operation manager, Mia Baker, and Sam Davis to keep the production of Wolfscape on track at Leavitt Peak Press.

PROLOGUE

The Edge

A pair of sky-blue eyes moved through the gloom intently. Studying the activities at the edge of the landing spot. The hulking gray figure, alone, and alert, was watching some kind of commotion in the brightly lit area next to the hospital. He wasn't sure how he arrived, only that he was concerned for his friend and somehow knew his friend would be coming. He and his friend had experienced a terrible ordeal. He had regretted that he couldn't do more for him when a huge gray wolf attacked him, because he had arrived too late and could only chase his "other" away. Looking on at his friend lying in the snow hurt, and bleeding, he was afraid to get too close. The next day, his friend had somehow managed to keep going only to fall into some kind of shaft while he had been helping him find his way. He had suspected his friend was looking for others of his kind, and he was leading him to the nearest town when the accident happened.

A black thing came out of the sky filling, his vision with uneasiness. Careful of not wanting to be seen, he retreated further away continuing to scan the scene. He missed his friend, longing for someone that didn't fear him, someone that looked past and accepted him for who he was. The black thing opened, and figures stepped out onto the snow, ducked, and withdrew from under the whirling blades. He knew by the scent these things were dangerous and not to be trifled with. A figure he recognized was brought out on some kind of structure and moved up the steps to the hospital. It was his friend. He still was frustrated that he couldn't do more for him. Even though his friend had been hurt from the accident, there should have been something more that he could have done, but he was afraid to get too close. Even his kind had already rebuffed him, and he wasn't sure if he could take another rejection. To his surprise, he didn't know who he was or what he had become, and he wasn't sure if he wanted to find out.

The black thing with the shiny blades was scary and noisy. It reminded him of a huge roaring black bear, but without the whirling things. He was curious why the figures didn't see him. He wasn't that far away. He wondered if he could see himself, but suspected he couldn't since others of his kind could not–only glimpses. He only knew when he was near; they mostly reacted out of fear.

He watched as others climbed the stairs. More shapes from the whirling thing stood around and now talking and gesturing to each other. The sound of their voices sliced through the atmosphere and echoed in his ears. He wondered what it was about. He hoped that his friend was okay. He had remembered staring down at his friend in a hole, watching him reaching and saying something. *What was he trying to say, and why was he reaching?* The creature was trying to remember. Could his kind remember? He wasn't sure. He wasn't even sure about when it had happened, only that it had occurred sometime after the splitting. He moved to get a better view and remembered that he had a difficult time helping his friend until an idea of a fallen tree limb came into his purview. He wasn't sure how this had happened; it had just appeared in his consciousness. Everything presented itself this way. Regardless of where he was or what he was doing, it always seemed that whenever he wanted something or to go somewhere it just happened. At first, it had shocked him, disorienting him knowing that it had been more than instinct. *But what was it?* Even his environment had changed. The landscape he traveled was strange and foreign, but at the same time exciting. Sound traveled more easily, his vision and hearing had become more acute–all his senses were tuned. It was as if he had added a sixth sense. He seemed stronger, faster and traveled wherever he wanted in a blink of an eye.

Some of the figures where now moving away from the whirling thing waving at others that were still there. He missed his kind. Communicating and posturing with them after the splitting had become more difficult. Sometimes, he thought they understood, but in the end, it had always been the same–confusion and fear. It was as though he could see through them and sometimes feel their instinct. He wasn't sure if cogency was in the neighborhood, but it was sure around the corner. He only knew that his old life had vanished, what life there was, and pain and fear were now in his purview.

The change had left him longing. Hunting in the wilderness with his kind, he was sure that he missed the camaraderie and companionship. *But where was his old life, and how long ago was it?* He knew it had been awhile since the splitting. At night, his thoughts always filled with bits and pieces and shades of fright from the events of that fateful day. Tumbling, visions off the edge, falling, grasping for something but always out of reach, fragments of images continued to haunt him. Understanding was always on the next block, and he could only guess why he had been in the fight of his life. *What was he fighting, and why was he fighting? Could beings of his kind dream?* He wasn't sure, but ever since that awful day, he knew he was different and could connect with others through his dreams.

The weather was changing, growing colder by the minute and wouldn't be long before snow paid its presence. It was time to leave, time to explore the canyons of his mind or instincts, or whatever he was looking for. As he flashed away, two of the men from the helo, Jim Hazelton and Humberto Sanchez looked up.

Jim could see twigs flying and branches moving through a thin veil of billowing snow.

"Did you see that?" Jim asked.

The shorter and stockier man turned to his friend shaking his head, staring at a vision he couldn't believe. "I'm not sure."

By now, Jim was searching with his powerful field glasses for the spot where his eyes had been. Catching movement, his brain couldn't comprehend what his eyes were seeing. "Holy crap, there it is again."

Bert looking at his friend, black eyes staring, with thoughts pulling at the corners of his mind, looking for some kind of recognition he knew wasn't there, answered, "I saw something but I can't explain it." By now, the other men in the group were peering in the distance, straining to see what Jim and Bert had seen.

With a faraway look in his brown eyes, Jim finally said, "It's the strangest thing." His voice trailed to a whisper, as if coming from somewhere else. "The…the tracks are still there, and then

nothing." His mind straining, searching for anything familiar. He drilled to the fire, the cougar attack, the earthquake, his dreams, the Derecho, and lastly, the wolf tracks disappearing in the snow two days ago. *Could it be?* He thought. He looked out to where the thing had been. He could clearly see tracks in the snow, leading to the thicket of Aspens grow shallower and then vanish altogether. Looking beyond, the ground was still moving with twigs flying and branches snapping, but where was the creature?

ONE

Telluride

The airliner slipped through the ridge line of the Rockies and vectored for its short, steep approach to Telluride Regional Airport. It had the distinction of being North America's highest commercial airfield at an elevation of 9,078 feet atop Deep Creek Mesa. The town and airport sat in a bowl ringed by the snow- covered San Juan Mountains, rising majestically four to five thousand feet above. The silver bird swayed and shuttered in the blizzard as it fought for its approach. The passengers had already been instructed to pull out their floatation devices from underneath the seats, place them in their laps, and lean forward. The plane descended toward the barely visible lighted runway, rolling, yawning, and pitching violently as it battled against wind sheer and powerful down drafts ricocheting across the valley.

Emergency lights flickered in the seesawing cabin; white LED aisle lights showing the way to the emergency exits. The engines droned, screaming, changing pitch as the plane fought against the elements. The cabin creaked, carry-ons flying about, and oxygen masks dropping and bouncing as passengers blanched with fear, trying to maintain their sensibilities. When the airliner touched down it skipped once, and then slapped hard against the tarmac with a horrific screech of its landing gear. Pilots struggling, the plane nearly skidded off the heated runway before coming to a stop.

Thirty minutes later, Frank and Alice Thompson, along with the flight crew and fellow passengers departed the plane. Some had injuries, and nearly all had headaches, pale faces, and trembling legs. They were herded into a makeshift debriefing room by airline personnel and then examined by the airport's medical staff. Afterward, Frank and Alice collected their luggage and presents and sat in a non-secured area of the terminal to relax, get their breath and take their medications.

"Hon, you still haven't gained your color and your breathing seems irregular. You okay?"

"I'm fine, babe. Just need to catch my breath from the high altitude. Need to get one of my inhalers out of the luggage." After using the device to calm his chronic asthma, Frank leaned over and had another coughing spell. *Maybe Alice was right, they shouldn't have taken this trip,* he thought. *After all this time, he still marveled at her musings on topics that he could barely fathom and, at the same time, doubted his doubts that she was intellectually superior to him.* Although at times he wondered if she was making sense about certain things. She was extremely intelligent, and that's probably the reason why she was diagnosed a year ago with a psychotic disorder. At least that's the way Frank understood it. All of the medical tests and definitions was a bit more than he could fathom. The doctors had recently switched her to Asenapine, which belongs to the class of drugs called atypical antipsychotics. It works by helping to restore the balance of certain natural substances in the brain, which are referred as neurotransmitters. Frank had suspected that Alice's thinking was a bit odd at times, and she would say or see things that just weren't there. And sometimes she would complain about movement when there wasn't any.

After a quick bite and collecting their rental Chevy Trailblazer, they headed to the local market for groceries and Christmas decorations. It was their first winter vacation away from the family, and they were excited about decorating their little place in the mountains. They were amazed at the lavish spectacle spread before them: an old mining town changing hats to a glitzy showcase lit up like a Christmas tree, activity everywhere with its fancy boutiques and fancy people glamorous in their ski gear. "You'd think we were at Santa's Village at the North Pole with all this sparkle. The kids would love it."

"Love it or not, we're already running late, and I want to get going. It could be a rough drive. We'll celebrate later," Frank said, eyeing the weather.

After loading provisions into the car and checking the vehicle's GPS, they headed to their remote get-a-way, tucked high in the mountains, twenty-two miles from civilization. The plane incident had caused them a two-hour delay, and they wanted to get there before nightfall.

My word. There are better ways starting a vacation, Alice thought. She turned to her husband and was about to say something and thought better of it after seeing his knuckles, white, clenching the steering wheel in a death grip. In silence, they listened to Christmas carols from their CD collection as the whine of the Blazer's overworked heating and defrosting system competed for their attention. Something more was competing: cold and unforgiving, the glint of death flashed on the horizon as the car headed down the snow-covered road toward their destination in the middle of December.

TWO

The Chase

The tracks were fresh, probably a small Rocky Mountain Mule Deer and alone. Why wasn't it with its band? Didn't appear to be hurt, not with its steady stride. He'd been tracking the animal for well over an hour as it wandered aimlessly among the Ponderosa pine and aspen. He thought about kill strategy, it was more instinct than cogency. He knew he was getting close, scent growing stronger as time went on, and hoofed tracks leading the way in the deep snow. No sightings yet, but he was confident he would soon see it. He thought about calling the others, but knew he could handle it himself. This should be easy as long as close comes his way. Perhaps he should circle around and wait until the prey comes to him, but he wasn't sure which route to take. The smell of pine kept interfering with his scent, and he was growing impatient with the ever-shifting wind. He was hungry. He and the others hadn't eaten since early yesterday morning.

He was still gaining the trust of the pack ever since the splitting. It seemed like they didn't trust him anymore, wary of him at every turn. He had arrived back to his home, hunting grounds three weeks ago after being gone for almost eight months. It was though they had left him for dead; didn't care anymore. He was much bigger and stronger then the rest, but there wasn't any respect, and he didn't like that. He knew that he had changed; he could see it in their eyes, looking at him differently as if he was an outlander. He would have to prove his worth, just like before, teaching them and using his superior hunting skills.

Just then, Rollo saw the large ears on the small buck perk up. The forked horn was standing near the crest of a hill above him. He was trying to stay down wind as much as possible, but the wind kept shifting, and he wasn't sure if he could continue to tack without being noticed. He needed to be still, keeping low, he hid behind one of the larger shrub pines. The waiting game began.

Still quiet, like leaves staying home on a windless day, he peeked through the lower branches of the big pine and could see the animal standing sideways behind an aspen, sniffing the air. Stealth, playing in the game, he slinked from pine to pine, keeping his eyes on the prize, forever mindful of the wind swirling among the spruce, pines, and aspens.

The winter dusk had settled two hours ago, and the shroud of darkness fell upon the valleys and mountaintops like a veil of silence. The air, colder and still moving, was frosty with sounds traveling easy among the gullies, rugged canyons, and mountainside. He now had the advantage. Close enough to sense fear and uneasiness; he focused his blue eyes on the ungulate.

The alpha was large for its kind; in fact, you could say huge at over 140 lbs. and tall at the shoulders. Challenge was never in Rollo's vocabulary even for larger felines. Blunt snout, canines gleaming with saliva, he surveyed the kill zone. Moving softly but steadily toward his target, he seemed almost relaxed, confident in his skills. Rising from the east, the winter moon cast a silvery glint on his gray, rough fur. His target was pacing, trying to pick up the scent of its predator as he crept closer. Guard hairs hackling around his shoulders, the wolf moved within striking range. The deer looked right at him, but fear blinded his sight, only sensing something at hand. Legs adjusting with muscles bunched, the night run struck with lightning speed. Gleaming jaws agape with fiery eyes, air was his enemy as he slammed into the spruce and ricocheted to the tree well. Crawling out, snout sore with bleeding triangular ears was not his concern. Where was his meal? He raced to the hill's crest, and off in the distance, snow billowing in clouds of white, he spotted the deer. Racing down the other side his only hope was misdirection or fatigue.

Fear in its veins and under its skin, steam shot from its nostrils. Lungs driven with air, it moved ever faster down the hillside barely missing tree wells and other obstacles. Uneven now in its stride, the deer needed to get somewhere, somewhere safe. Slowing, deep in snow and adrenaline no longer a friend, terror, challenging instinct, not out of choice but out of necessity, it waited.

THREE

The Ride

The falling snow intensified the further Frank drove from town, and Alice noticed the trees seemed more scraggly and stunted as they gained elevation. *It must be the cold and altitude,* she thought. She took a hanky from her coat pocket, wiping the side window clear of condensation and ice, she looked out. Through the gloom, she could see the roadway's orange snow poles buried at eight feet.

Turning off the main highway onto Mountain Way Road, Frank put the Blazer in low range, four-wheel drive. He knew this was the most treacherous part of the trip from their summer visits. The road narrowed as the car crawled along switchbacks, traveling on a ribbon of ice winding into the clouds. Alice sat curled in her seat. Even though the plow's snow bank had partially blocked her sight, she was grateful for the cloud deck obscuring her view to the valley below—vertigo was her enemy. Alice hoped that Frank was hugging the mountainside of the road. She couldn't take it much longer and finally turned with panic in her voice. "Let's turn back and stay in town; weather's frightful."

"Naw, honey, we're almost there. We'll be fine."

"Are you sure? Snow's coming down in sheets. I just don't know…" Alice grew quiet, fear challenging reason in her seat as they traveled further up the mountain, heading straight into the white wilderness.

Turning onto High Valley Lane, leading to their hideaway, Frank suddenly stopped the Blazer.

"What's wrong, dear?"

"Look straight ahead through the windshield, hon." "What is that, Frank?" Just looking at the animal, Alice shivered with fear. It was huge and nearly all gray with white guard hairs around its neck. But what caught Alice's attention the most were the eyes. They were sky blue and mesmerizing. Alice felt as though she was in a trance, asking for what the creature wanted.

"If I didn't know any better, I'd say it's a gray wolf and a big guy at that."

"Do wolves get that large, hon?" Alice asked as she continued to stare with alarm at the beast.

"Not usually. I'd say we are looking at a 140-pound animal.

And those eyes, I've never seen eyes like that before on any animal. They both peered through the windshield, caught up in their own imaginations as the car's headlights reflected the creature's eyes back at them. The animal seemed regal; standing there, but at the same time exuded an air of haughtiness seldom seen in the animal kingdom. As it backed into the white curtain still staring at them and disappeared into the wilderness, Alice and Frank sat in stunned silence. A chilling pall came over them as they tried to comprehend the vision of what they had just seen. In silence, Frank put the Blazer back in gear and continued on. They were now on relatively flat terrain, and the road was recently plowed, true to the rental car agency's information. It was one of the extra services the area offered in the high country.

Nightfall fell and placed its icy grip upon the snowy landscape. With intense brown eyes, Frank peered through the car's windshield. Past the snow-crusted wipers, he could see the reflection of ice crystals glistening like diamonds fading in the night to a crystalline curtain's gossamer edges of the car's headlamps, and feel the crunch of snow beneath the tires. *Thank God for the car's GPS.* He thought. *Otherwise, they would never find the place.* He wanted Alice in good cheer, and without turning, said, "come on, honey, where's your sense of adventure? After we unload, I'll start a fire and fix some hot chocolate—it'll be fun."

With danger flying on the wings of testosterone, Frank drove on. Even though the Blazer had all four corners shod with chains, it had taken more than two hours to drive twenty-two miles to reach their snow covered alpine cabin five hundred feet below the tree line at eleven thousand feet.

Normally, they had used their digs as a summer hide-away. Both were raised and lived in Wilmington, North Carolina. Alice, on a whim, had purchased the cabin from her elderly parents three years ago. Built in the 1940s by the federal government, the outpost served as a weather and fire platform until it was auctioned to private enterprise in 1970. Small and primitive in amenities, the wood structure adjacent to some very old Bristlecone pines came with two rooms, drafty windows, and an old wood-burning fireplace. The small alcove kitchen with its two-burner propane stove and a small oven had been added almost as an afterthought, and the indoor plumbing barely met the definition. An old fuse box from a bygone era met the cabin's electrical needs. Code wise the place was a disaster, but the vacation home had met their needs, or so they thought.

Deciding something different this year, they vacationed in the winter. A grand holiday it was, sixteen days at the cabin with New Year's Eve in Telluride, and then off to Mexico for two weeks. Neither one had much exposure or experience to harsh winter climates, though Frank knew how to drive in snow from his studies at Mt. Washington during his college years–just enough to get them in trouble. At first, she had tried to talk her husband out of the winter recreation idea because of their physical condition. Both in their mid-forties, prematurely gray, and couch potatoes in search of a good exercise program, Frank had finally convinced her this ticket would break them out of their rut.

Chopping wood and shoveling snow would be good, he had told her. Alice had finally relented and now found herself waking to the seventh dawn of their sixteen-day stay. She was excited.

Christmas morning had finally arrived, and she was looking forward to exchanging gifts and cooking a nice ham dinner for her husband. Frank had been a sweetheart, helping decorate and going out and finding just the right Colorado blue spruce for their Christmas tree. But she needed her gold-colored mukluks; the cabin floor was ice cold.

Snowfall had been steady ever since they arrived, changing yesterday to ice pellets. Their constant companion, the wind, howled and danced its swirl through the bleak landscape of stunted Colorado spruce, pine, and aspen as it drove the snowdrifts ever higher. The temperature had fallen the last two days, and now had found a friend at negative ten.

Her toes grew colder by the minute. Surely, her mukluks would warm her feet, but where were they? *I know,* she thought, *they're under the bed.* She gingerly knelt on all fours and poked her head below the box spring, and sure enough, that's where they were. Her bones creaked from arthritis as she put the winter boots on the bed. Considering how to rise, she placed both hands flat on top the bed for support, and struggled as she hauled herself to an upright position. *Lordy!* She thought. *Eight thirty in the morning and she had already broken a good sweat.* She needed to exercise; they both did, and then swore under her breath. Damn husband, always kicking her shoes out of reach. Next time, she's going to get even and hide his long johns. See if he likes being out here without underwear. She giggled.

"What's that, honey?" Frank asked, walking out of the bathroom. Wolverines in hand, he stumbled across the cold floor trying to put them on.

"I said, do we have enough wood to get us through the next nine days? And how's the car? Will it start? You better check it, and if it doesn't, we could be in trouble."

Frank looked sideways at his wife with her blue eyes and bleached, grayish-blonde morning hair. "How come you're so concerned? I'm sure it'll start. Besides, if it doesn't, we can call for help."

"No, we can't."

Finally pulling on his boots, he asked, "What do you mean?"

"Honey, I forgot to bring the charger. I tried the phone last night to check on the kids, and it didn't work–no bars. Anyway we probably have no reception; not in this weather."

Turning to Alice while running a meaty hand through his coarse gray hair, he looked at her again. "The phone battery probably drained faster than normal because of the cold and the cabin's primitive heating system. Been running through wood just to keep the chill off." Lacing his boots, he shook his head, ran through his options and bellowed, *"Damn, Alice! Why did you forget the charger? You knew about the winter conditions up here, didn't you?"*

"Don't get on me about forgetting things and winter conditions. You knew I didn't want to go. You knew we weren't experienced, and out of shape for this," she glowered, placing her hands on her full hips.

"Ok, ok, I get the point. How much dry wood do we have?"

"Look for yourself, you know where it's at," she barked.

He turned and looked at the firewood rack next to the fireplace, and could see there was enough for a couple of days. He knew he could cut more out back, but it was damp and wouldn't burn very well. Besides, he was growing tired of splitting wood; his hands were blistered from the effort. Splitting mauls were not his friend. "Looks like there's enough to heat the cabin for another four or five days, and then I'll have to cut more." He didn't want to alarm her.

"Great, that's all we need."

"Honey, everything will be fine. You'll see." Frank donned his gray North Face winter coat; leather gloves and ski cap and headed out to the Blazer. It was like walking into a maelstrom.

Relentless in its pain, ice needles rode the North winds searching for its prey.

While her husband was outside, she looked around the cabin's interior. Seeing the opaque windows, what windows they had, iced with rime from the inside, she heard ice crystals bang off them like the sound of crinkling cellophane. Just looking at them made her shiver. *Place should have been updated years ago.* Alice took stock of their food supply and determined they had eight or nine days left, consuming at their present rate. They could probably stretch it to two weeks. *No problem with water*, she reasoned. *If only she could trade snow for food and heat.*

Clearing ice and snow from the driver's door, Frank slid in and tried the ignition. Nothing, totally dead. Then he thought, *Oh my God! I made a fatal mistake. Instead of facing the Blazer's front end away from the wind, it was pointing straight into it. Besides the battery being dead, the engine block had probably frozen solid.* He stepped out and cleared snow and ice from the car's front end, found the latch, and lifted the hood. With great effort, he twisted off the radiator cap, and poked his gloved index finger inside, and met nothing but solid ice. His worst nightmare had come alive. He knew, now, that Alice was right. *Bit late,* he thought.

FOUR

The Pack

The alpha's howling alerted the wolf pack. They were sheltered in a grove of aspens, and all ears pointed toward the howls as they tried for the scent. There were five of them, a smaller omega, two females, and two pups. Like no other, the sound they heard ricocheted and rolled in waves across the frozen expanse, not like an echo but something unnatural. Two voices, one moment in harmony, the next in staccato singularity, both different in tone and in pitch. The group huddled together looking at each other, and then peered into the expanse. The omega finally stepped forward, raised his head, and with a throaty howl, signaled for what he thought was the alpha's call. Hunger driving them, they cautiously moved out of the grove, heading toward the sound. In front of them, the scent already confirmed what they knew. Another unholy howl erupted across the valley guiding them to the kill.

The ungulate, lying on its side, paralyzed, twisted, and bleeding out, rattled its final call. Rising air, mixing with steam, and a thick coppery stench, it saw its final vision–a huge gray shadowy figure, fangs bared with saliva and blood dripping and those fiery blue eyes. The snow, now red, imparted a grizzly scene as the alpha stood sentry, waiting for his family. Rollo wasn't going to eat. Not yet. Social and caring within their pack, the night run patiently waited, pacing around its victim, securing the site, and scenting the air for nearby predators. He was bothered by the vision of blue eyes and shifting needle-like fur off in the distance while howling for the others. The eyes seemed to haunt him as a strange cry joined his signaling for the pack. *But how could this be?*

Scenting again, he could feel those strange sky blue eyes piercing and that strange sound emanating from somewhere beyond. The big alpha was getting spooked. He paced and scented around the deer for a third time just to make sure. After deciding, there was no danger, he reclined next to the deer after seeing that familiar look. Brown eyes staring, glazed over, the wolf knew there would be no more challenge. Ears pointed as sound traveled from the omega, he signaled once again, and once again he heard that strange cry rumbling through the valley. Impatient in his desire, he doubted hunger could remain at bay much longer.

Seeing the pack in the distance with the young omega in the lead, pups, and females closing ranks, Rollo was excited for their arrival. With a nip and friendly nuzzle, he tried greeting his old mate, but she was having none of it. Begrudgingly he acknowledged the others. They weren't particularly glad to see him either, except for the kill he provided. His patience was waning, and he wasn't sure how much longer he could hold off his hunger. The pack, hungry too, was ready to get their work done and slake their appetites. Holding hunger back, the big alpha did a peculiar thing. He allowed the younger and much smaller omega to go first. The younger wolf whined at first, not knowing what to do until the alpha nodded toward the kill. After finishing, the smaller omega looked back, and with a soft command, he signaled the others to join. After everyone had finished, they turned to go as the big wolf finally took his turn.

For wolves, it's either feast or famine, and even though they are relentless and efficient hunters and good stewards of their environment, energy is critical in their success and is often hard to come by, especially in the winter. For their kind, contrary to the beliefs of man, the carnivores are shy by nature and will only attack humans under extreme need or provocation.

Afterward, the big alpha followed the pack back to the aspens for a well-deserved rest, all the while thinking of his next kill. He used to be their leader, the patriarch of the family, always at the ready to guide, protect, and serve. What had happened?

The change must have been significant. After settling down a way from the group and before sleeping, he noticed the pack's attention was focused up hill and away from the grove. Something was riveting their interest; he didn't care; he was tired. As he drifted toward slumber they listened as "blue eyes" told them the adventures of the Great White Wolf of the North. Their ears perked in attention as they learned from their leader. Later, they dreamed of their own escapades with the great creature from the north.

FIVE

Tracks

Walking back to the cabin, Frank spotted animal tracks off to the right. Following them to a steep slope a quarter of a mile away, he knelt and looked closely at them. Before disappearing down the embankment, the two smaller pairs had split off in another direction from the larger pair. The larger ones appeared to be that of a cougar or another member of the feline family. He had remembered the other night waking to a child's scream. At first, confused, it gradually dawned on him that it must have been a big cat. He kept it to himself, not wanting to frighten Alice. The other prints looked like coyotes but larger. He knew coyote tracks all right, he had seen them in the countryside around Wilmington when bird hunting with his friends. "*Wolves,*" he said to himself. He had read somewhere that gray wolves were now migrating south along the Rockies. *But why we're all three so close together?* He thought. Wolves and cougars don't mix. Either the tracks were made at different times, and he couldn't discern from the condition of them in the snow, or one predator was stalking the other–he couldn't tell.

Standing with his shoulder to the wind, he looked across the valley from the edge of the embankment to see if he could spot more of them off in the distance. There appeared to be some older tracks, but he wasn't sure what kind they were. As he continued to look, he marveled at the landscape before him. He knew the high mountain valley was at least two miles wide, but today it had disappeared into a white curtain of snow and ice less than a quarter mile out. The wind was still raging from the north and he could feel the ice pellets assaulting him from the side. He turned and walked to the Blazer, stooping along the way to collect his orange markers that he had placed on his way out to the slope. After arriving back to the car, he took a moment to catch his breath while looking around for other tracks. He was worried about the added danger of predators being nearby.

When packing for the trip, he never thought about bringing his father's old handgun. It was an old wheel gun, a Smith & Wesson 38 Police Special that his dad used during his days of being a law enforcement officer in Wilmington. The gun wouldn't be much protection beyond fifty feet, but at least it would've been something. He knew that he and Alice were in serious trouble, and decided to break the news to his wife gently. Lord knows she was already upset with their circumstances.

He came tromping back inside, breathing heavily and full of ice. Turning and looking at him, right away, Alice could sense trouble in his ice encrusted, bearded face. "What's wrong dear?"

"The car won't start."

SIX

Charlie

T he little omega missed his friend. Sometimes at night and especially while scavenging, he caught flashes of him from behind. It was almost like he was being followed and guided. Ever since the disappearance, he was responsible for his pack mates.

Survival had always been slim this time of year, but with the big fella gone it was more difficult. It had been eight months since he had last seen him, but his presence never left. Three weeks ago, Rollo had suddenly arrived back out of the blue. Gone for all those months he somehow seemed different. Charlie sensed that his friend had changed, he was sullen and moody at times, and even though he was his companion, Charlie didn't trust him anymore. He looked bigger, stronger with those blue eyes piercing through him, able to see things that he could only see. Behind those eyes, he could sense a haunting, chilling to the bone. It was cold and unyielding, and he was afraid, never knowing if Rollo was an adversary or a friend.

Traversing the steep slope above the box canyon, the little wolf tilted his head to scent the damp, winter air. He could tell the pine, spruce, and juniper wasn't as dominate as it was a few days ago. Junipers always jumped his scent when conditions were drier. The wind obeying, once again became his friend. As always, he was hunting, and the harsh climate continued to challenge his skills. He was proud of his eyesight.

His gold-yellow eyes could focus well beyond the normal range of his canid brethren and sometimes he could spot field mice two hundred feet ahead before picking up their scent, depending on the wind. As acute as his vision was, his ungainly gait posed significant challenges, and more than once, his eyesight came to the rescue. His legs were simply too long.

Foraging along, he noticed a thicket of brush and aspen on a sharp rise above him and saw movement. Too late! The big cat was on him in a blink of an eye. The wolf rolled, avoiding the full impact as the cat skidded past him. Regaining his balance, the omega bounded up the rise toward the stand of aspens. The feline snarled in surprise, seeing the wolf heading for her cubs. With murder in her sandy colored eyes, the big gray cat bounded after its prey. At the top, the wolf turned swiftly, bared his fangs, and faced his adversary. He had the high ground. The cougar stopped suddenly, cocked her ears as if listening for something. In all the excitement, the omega didn't see the two young cubs at his feet. He knew he was in mortal danger, but this bought him some time.

Ears flattened the mountain devil snarled and screamed, but the wolf held its ground and wouldn't be intimidated. The element of surprise was wasted, spent like a discharging firearm; there would be no second chance for this bullet. It was negotiation time. The cat had two choices, either a direct frontal assault –chancy with her two cubs nearby, or a stealth attack from the trees. The cougar prowled slowly up the rise, eyeing the omega warily; ready to bunch her muscles for the spring of death. The silver devil stopped again, pitched her head to the side, and screamed. What was it? The wolf heard it too–growling and hissing off in the distance. The big cat now spooked–sensed something was stalking her. She didn't care; she had to get to her cubs. With one last glance behind, she sprang. The delay was enough for the omega to step aside and avoid a direct hit. With a glancing blow the feline shot past with the night run now on its back, ripping at the big cat's neck. They rolled in the snow, the wolf clamping down with its powerful jaws, searching for the jugular with its canines. The snow turning red, and the cougar continued to roll with its powerful body, trying to shed its prey. The wolf dug in with its claws, clenching the cat's powerful hindquarters and its upper neck with its forepaws. Driving its canines deeper into the cat's neck, the cougar screamed again. The snow, a bright crimson now, the omega shredded and ripped the cougar's jugular with its incisors exploding blood into the air and to the ground. It was over. There was nothing to do but hang on as life drained from the big cat. It was up close and personal, like it always had been and always will be. It was the wolf's biggest kill, and it wasn't even planned. How did he manage, and why did the big cat hesitate?

Again, he felt the presence of something around him as he rolled in the snow to clean himself. The shock of the encounter having subsided, he stepped to the edge of the rise, and with a lusty howl he called to the pack. His muscles were sore, and bruises were welling on his back and sides from taking the weight of the big cat. Nothing he couldn't handle. After all, he was Charlie, the meanest omega around, and now he was becoming an alpha. And then there were bragging rights, not to mention a fine meal. He howled again.

SEVEN

The Splitting

Rollo could sense trouble ahead. He hadn't been in this area ever since that fateful day. He had remembered chasing a marmot, closing in for the kill when something stepped out of the brush and then nothing. Later, coming to, he felt the ground move under him as if something was dragging him. It was large, and in the shape of a bear. Twisting, turning, and growling, he had somehow freed himself and lunged at the creature, trying for its throat. The bruin had grabbed him in a bear hug, digging its massive claws deep into his side. Rollo had yelped and remembered clenching the upper body of the omnivore with his fore paws and, sinking his canines deep into its neck; the bear had let out a mighty roar. They had been locked in a life and death struggle. Who would relent first, the black bear or the wolf? As blood gushed from the bear's throat, they had fallen to the ground, rolling down an incline. The weight of the bruin and its claws were crushing, but Rollo hung on and bit deeper into the bear's neck. Roaring at first, the sound had changed to a barking noise and then a whimper as the two continued to slide and thrash down the hill. At the bottom, the bear had relaxed its hold on the wolf as it took the full brunt of a huge boulder, shielding the wolf from the impact. When the bear hit, Rollo heard a loud snapping sound from the head of the omnivore, like bones jacking deep inside vertebrae, and he had been suddenly released. He had rolled off the bear, bruised, battered, and bleeding heavily. He couldn't move, and had been paralyzed by exhaustion and weak from the loss of blood. He had remembered lying motionless, thirsty, and in agony that seemed to go on for days. After a long while, he had managed to stand and hobble to a nearby creek to attend his wounds. It was there, lying in the creek bed, that he had experienced even more pain and suffering. He was on fire, ensconced in the flames of hell, the next, freezing on the plains of Patagonia. He had railed against the extremes, morphing into something from within. Rollo had watched in horror, retching from the pain not believing his eyes or his instincts of what was happening in front of him. An outline was emerging from him or was it from the water–he couldn't tell. It was wolf like, but even larger than himself with its fur shimmering, translucent in the moon glow–gray but silver at the same time. The thing rising to its full height was now standing over him in the shallow creek bed, partially shadowed by the moon behind–its silver-gray fur hackling around its shoulders and along its flanks, needle like. Its blue eyes shined the fires of hell, wavering and staring at him as saliva dripped from its huge jaws, splashing silver-like to the water below. In the next instant, it had moved to the creek's bank, turned and peered at him as if beseeching him. But what, what was he supposed to do? He had remembered when he looked again, the creature was gone–vanished as if it had never been.

Only the sound of its unholy howl was left behind. Crawling to the bank himself, he had lied on the ground for what seemed like hours. By dawn, he had fully regained his strength and was healed. The pain and the hurt had left, like flower blossoms floating away on a windy day. The transformation had been remarkable and complete.

By that afternoon, with the sun playing peek-a-boo with the clouds, he had regained his appetite. He was famished. It hadn't been long before he found himself tracking a feral hog, and it was a big one. With his newfound strength and agility, he had taken down and killed the animal faster than anything he had ever done before in his life. He had been surprised by the ferocity of his attack and the quickness of the kill. His appearance had changed, he was larger, stronger, and more confident, but his personality and temperament had fused to an ugly mess of meanness and spitefulness. He was still Rollo, but different. By now the bear attack was a tattered piece of his past, but not the creature, and somehow he knew that they would cross paths again.

Decision

Before she could speak, Frank waved her off. He needed to catch his breath, sit, and relax. He reached to the small end table, collected his inhaler and took a long pull. Dark thoughts were rolling across his mind like waves crashing on a distant shore. Terror and foreboding gripping as he fought for options for their survival. He motioned to Alice.

"What are we going to do, Frank? I mean, won't people come looking for us in a few days. I'm sure we have enough wood and supplies to last until help arrives."

"I don't know, honey. Remember, we're not due back for another twenty-four days."

"*Oh, God*. That's right. We are supposed to fly out on January 3rd, to Puerto Vallarta for two weeks. We're in trouble, aren't we?"

"I think so."

Alice began to pace the small room, mentally inventorying their supplies. She knew they had enough food for at least a week–probably longer. But she was worried about fuel–the wood. There was still a small supply of dry wood in the lean to out back, but it wasn't enough. Sure, there were trees around, but the wood would be damp and wouldn't burn well. Besides, Frank's hands were already blistered, and he had a bad back. She turned, and with her blue eyes blazing, she shrieked, "I told you we shouldn't have done this, and now we might die!"

"Alice, will you get a hold of yourself?" Frank huffed. "We need to figure out our options and then make a decision." Frank stood and peered at one of the small, opaque windows. "Have you tried the cell phone again?"

"Of course. I tried while you were outside checking the car.

The phone is dead, so we can rule out that option. What's the weather like outside?"

"You don't want to know," Frank said, still looking at the window and hearing ice drumming off the panes. He knew what the weather was like, and without any form of communication and only a little propane and wood, they were now thrown nearly back to the nineteenth century–not much comfort there. *Propane.* He thought. Maybe he could rig a line to the fireplace–iffy at best and dangerous, too. Was there extra line; he would check.

Otherwise, they could get some heat from the two-burner propane stove. Not much, but anything would help. "Alice, we need to do a check list and run through it–we can't miss a thing."

His wife turned and walked into the bedroom to retrieve her purse while Frank moved closer to one of the small windows and stared out at the bleak landscape. Seeing what he could, the old windows didn't help much, and he could feel the cold. Now that he was warmer from the fireplace, he took off his gloves and cap and shrugged out of his coat. The ice pooled around him on the rough-hewn wood floor like water standing on pavement.

After Alice returned, they both sat on the couch. She writing while her husband ran through the options, fidgeting with his thick hands. Afterward, she made hot chocolate while Frank donned his coat and went out back to check the wood and propane and to see if there was enough line, tools, and supplies to jerry-rig the wood fireplace. There wasn't, and the wood and propane were lower than he thought. He now knew there was only one option left, and he only hoped that the weather would cooperate and give him a fighting chance. His next order of business was trying to charge the cell phone from whatever residual life was left from the Blazer's battery. *Good luck*, he thought. Though, this could give him another option. There wasn't any reception in or around the cabin, especially in these conditions, but he knew if the weather broke, he might get reception a mile or two down the mountainside–he could only hope.

After returning inside, he gave Alice the news. She leveled her blue eyes at him in horror and said, "You can't walk out of here. It's too far, and besides you'll freeze to death."

Frank took another sip of his hot chocolate, savoring the taste, and thought about what he would say next. "Honey, I have a plan, and if the weather cooperates in the next day or two, I think we'll be fine."

Alice went about fixing their Christmas dinner while he continued to sip on his hot chocolate. While putting the ham in the oven, she thought, *this might be the last decent meal we have in some time–might as well enjoy it.*

Frank looked at the list again to make sure there wasn't anything he missed. Actually, they were better prepared than he initially thought. Now that he could think clearly after the panic had subsided, he remembered that he had packed his old canvas bag full of camping gear. He wasn't sure, but he thought there was a nine-inch serrated-edged hunting knife; complete with a scabbard and a small whetstone. *Perfect.* He knew there were other camping items as well, such as metal tent stakes, waterproof container of matches and a Leatherman tool. He would give himself more time to rest before making another trip to the Blazer. He only wished that he was in better shape–twenty-two miles by road, or roughly fifteen miles cross country, wasn't going to be easy. A compass would have been nice.

Alice came over and sat next to him after attending to the ham and doing some prep work. "What are we going to do, honey?" She asked with a worried look in her blue eyes.

"I'm going out to the Blazer to see if I can get any charge for the cell phone from the car's battery, and check on the contents in the canvas tote. If I remember, I have some items that will be useful if I have to go for help."

"Even if you get the phone charged, it won't do us any good–we can't get reception up here."

"I'm not thinking up here, sweetheart. I'm thinking further down the mountain. I remembered we passed some cell towers on the way up. Even if I only get a few seconds of usage, I think the towers will pick up the phone's GPS coordinates. If we are still marooned up here, family will start checking in a few days, especially if they can't reach us in Mexico. The authorities will not only have the location of the cabin, but will have the time and date of our last transmission."

"Won't that be confusing?" Alice asked, shaking her head. "How's that?"

Alice got up and went to the small alcove to do more preparation. "I mean, they may check the area on the mountain from the last call and waste time before they come up here."

Frank scratched his short, graying beard in a thoughtful manner. "Hon, there may be some delay, but I highly doubt it. Besides, it will confirm are last time and date. As of now, the last time we were seen or heard was when we were in town, and that's been a week ago."

"I suppose you're right. I'm sure the kids or someone from the family will check on us soon."

"I'm sure they will. I'm going out to the blazer again and see if I can get some charge on the phone and get the bag, and anything else I think might be useful." Frank slipped on his coat, gloves and his RedHead cap, and threw an old scarf around his thick neck. *God, he hated going out again.* But he had no choice. Alice continued to fix Christmas dinner. Her hands were shaking.

NINE

Surprise

Anxiety and panic having left hours ago, Frank waded back into the maelstrom, fighting to reach the Blazer. Snow, deeper now, wind the sound of a freight train driving ice pellets into his face, he thought, *how would he ever get down the mountainside to test the phone, let alone making it to town. It was a reach!*

After scraping snow and ice from the rear, he grabbed the tailgate with both hands and pulled. It wouldn't budge. He got a better grip and slid behind his effort; still the same result. He finally gave up, and got back inside, and moved to the rear of the vehicle and flipped on his flashlight. The canvas bag was there. He moved it to the front along with the tire iron and a couple of blankets. He was thinking what he would use to help get him down the mountain–*snow was much too deep for any extended travel.*

Then it hit him. *If he could cut the spare tire in pieces, he could fashion snowshoes.* He tilted his cap to get a better view, planning as he went. He plugged in the phone, and while waiting he dug into the bag, and to his surprise, he found two value packs of chemical hand warmers– enough for his hands and feet. He was buoyed; things were looking up. He'd check the phone later.

He collected his find and headed toward the cabin, looking for fresh animal tracks along the way–there wasn't any. *Good.* He stumbled through the door in a cape of ice and dropped his catch in the middle of the room. Half frozen, he donned his outerwear moving toward the fireplace. Alice, sitting on the couch, stood and asked him if the phone was charging.

"I don't know yet. I'll check on it later. I want to see what's in this bag." Frank stepped to the canvas bag, kneeled, and pawed through the contents, laying them out as he went. Surveying the stash carefully, he was mighty glad that he packed it before leaving on their vacation. While Alice attended to dinner, he continued rummaging through his find. He had everything he thought he had packed, including small rope and even some visquene.

"Ready for dinner, hon?" Alice was bringing the fixings to the small table next to the alcove. "Might be the best meal we have in some time, so let's enjoy it."

It was midafternoon, and Frank was hungry. Hot chocolate didn't cut it. After dinner, he helped Alice with the dishes before going outside to check on the cell phone. They still had gifts to unwrap, but somehow it didn't feel right. Joy had left the little cabin, tucked in the mountains, and was replaced by the gift of dread.

Frank clawed his way outside again and had to practically break the driver's door to get inside. It had already iced up since leaving earlier. Once inside, he checked the phone for a charge. No such luck–nothing! Coming back inside, Alice asked the same question and Frank gave his answer.

"What are we going to do?" Alice asked with grave concern written across her face.

"Nothing, for now." Frank said. He didn't want to cause any undue alarm or panic. He could sense his wife already knew the answer, and they might as well enjoy the rest of the evening opening their presents. They would worry about it tomorrow–time was still on their side with food and fuel. After opening their gifts and having some hot toddies, they turned in early, not knowing their plight but hoping for the best tomorrow.

TEN

The Feast

Charlie howled again. He was getting impatient for the pack to show. They wouldn't believe the kill. He was so proud.

By now the two cubs had run off. He had given them only a short time to grieve the loss of their mother and treated them roughly to hasten their retreat. Ordinarily, they would have been on the menu. His instincts had never betrayed him, but lately he had been overcome by a presence so odd that it was almost alien. It was as if he was adding a sixth sense to his being, a feeling becoming so natural that it might diminish his other instincts and cause him to become more vulnerable. What was it he had wondered? Contrary to common sense, he was getting stronger, faster, and clumsy was becoming part of his past–no longer legged Charlie. He was more confident; reaching game he never knew he had the capacity for. But the feeling that came over him felt surreal, even bizarre.

He seemed to be operating on a different plane–a higher level of purpose with a stronger skill set, clarity, and a driving instinct to protect his family and himself.

Judging by their size, he guessed the cubs were four or five months old, on the cusp of surviving in the wilderness. He wished them well, though the odds as low as they were; best chance was given to an early exit. The winds of luck would decide their fate.

He could now see the pack off in the distance, running through the deep snow. The lead female stopped and howled, as the scent of the kill grew stronger. She could see a lone gray figure standing on the rise above her. Charlie circled the dead cat once more and scented for nearby predators; there were none. He stood at the crest of the hill, greeting the pack. As they congregated around, they looked at him with new-found pride and signaled for him to begin. As hungry as they were, they knew now that he was the lead alpha, sitting at the head of the table, taking his due. After they finished, Charlie led them, dragging the carcass from the kill site to the thicket of aspens in hopes of getting another meal. He wasn't worried about the pups; they were well past fending for themselves. After marking, the rest of the pack circled the site, still not believing what Charlie had done. They were amazed at his skill, or was it luck. How could a wolf of his size take down such a large creature? They noticed something different about him. He was bigger, apparently stronger, and more mature. Perhaps it was more about his age than anything else.

After awhile, they bedded down in the grove of aspens for a well-deserved rest. The Wolf Moon rising from the east witnessed the chaining of hearts as Charlie and the younger female, Lela, led the pack in proud camaraderie back to their den.

ELEVEN

Caterwaul

S creams seeping through the seams of her dream, Alice awoke with a start. She had been dreaming of a murder of ravens circling and cawing. But what were they seeing, what was the commotion? And now their harsh cries had turned to screams. *How can this be*, she thought as she fought for consciousness. It sounded almost like a child. Was there someone outside? She nudged her husband.

"Frank, you awake?" No response. She poked him harder. "What, what is it?" He asked, crawling from a deep sleep. "Did you hear the screams?"

"No, what was it?" Frank was getting irritated. Still suffering from too many hot toddies the night before, he just wanted to sleep.

In a vituperative manner, she kicked him hard. "Get your ass out of bed and check it out. I think someone's screaming outside."

Frank swung his legs to the edge, and with effort, stood on the ice-cold floor.

"There, you hear it?" It was a shrill, high-pitched sound—someone or something in agony. Tumbling, it appeared to be coming closer, and Alice was growing more concerned by the second.

He ran a meaty hand through his disheveled, gray hair thinking for a moment, trying to gain full consciousness. Pain darting between his brown eyes, he shot back, "Alice, it's a cougar."

"You sure?"

"Well, what else could it be? It's certainly not a group of children standing at our door, screaming to let them in." Even though he was still clearing cobwebs, Frank could see his wife was frightened. "Honey, we're fine. Probably a couple of big cats fighting outside."

She looked at her husband with more alarm, and Frank could tell he probably should rephrase it. "I bet it's a cat chasing something. I'll give it a check." He switched on the bed lamp and went to the alcove to fetch his hunting knife and then moved to one of the small, opaque windows in the cabin's main room and listened. His eyes had finally adjusted, and he peered out. *What is the sense in this*, he wondered. But then he heard something off in the distance. The wind had lessened yesterday, making sound less distorted. He heard it again. The unmistakable sounds of howling drifting on the currents of the air. And now another scream–much louder. He jumped with knife in hand–they needed to get out of here.

"Frank, did you hear that?" Alice's voice now in a whisper, mixing alarm with panic, asked again.

"It's only a cat, dear." Frank knew better. It was wolves fighting with a big cat. He needed to get help. Their window of opportunity was sliding close. No one had come in the last five days while he prepared and waited for the weather to clear. Why would he think otherwise? They were still early in their vacation and knowing their teenage daughter and son, why would they call. He half wished that there was a calamity brewing at home, something that would cause their kids to call and call repeatedly. Maybe they would call their uncle, and he would have the sense to call the authorities. *Wishful thinking,* he thought.

Actually their kids were really great. Jenny was a junior in high school with nearly perfect grades and waiting for the day that she would be admitted into medical school. If only he had her ambition at her age. Being a tire salesman hadn't brought him much comfort other than the fact it helped support the family. Jeffery was entirely different, excelling in sports and not caring about academics had brought new challenges to the family. Even though his son was good at football and track, was it enough to get him a college scholarship. He still had three years of high school left, and time would tell. In the meantime, he was relegated to constantly fighting with his son about the merits and balance between academics and sports.

Frank turned his thoughts back to the present–that's where he needed to be–their life depended on it and worried he was. Their fuel and food were getting lower by the day, and he hoped there was enough to get them through. With great effort he had managed to make snowshoes out of the Blazer's spare tire without butchering his hands–a minor miracle considering the tools at hand. He had already used them twice, once siphoning gasoline out of the Blazer in an old gas can. He was planning on using the extra fuel for burning wet wood if he had to, a chancy proposition at best, but one that gave him very little choice. The weather had been improving the last couple of days, and if it continued, he'd be on his way by the first of the year. It may take him up to five days to reach Telluride, and he hoped Alice would be okay without him. The phone was worthless, and they weren't expected home until after their Mexican vacation on the 18th–of January. There just wasn't any other way than to walk out. He had checked his gear, too many times to count, going over everything. He was ready. Now, if only the weather would cooperate.

TWELVE

Leaving Home

Dawn came easy on the first day of the New Year, unlike the difficulties that lie ahead. Wind had forgotten its song among the aspens, pines, and spruce, and the trees stood tall and straight. The temperature had risen the last few days and seemed almost warm at twenty-five degrees. Alice was in the alcove early before the crack of dawn, fixing her husband the last warm meal he would have in some time. Scraps of ham, pork, stale bread, and their last egg greeted Frank as he stepped out of the bathroom to the small table. His wife had already packed sandwiches with whatever fixings she could find. Their food store was depleted except for a few items that Alice would survive on waiting for her husband to bring help. Frank was in a somber mood, thinking about the trek in front of him. At least the weather had broken, and this is all he needed for a fighting chance to Telluride.

"Hon, I wish there was more." Alice said, sitting down next to her husband and handing him his last cup of coffee. She pulled at her hair, fretting about what would happen to him out in the wilderness. She was worried. Other things that came to her mind now seemed trivial, like the time he disappeared and didn't come home for three days. It had been a long time ago when Jeffery and Jenny were little. She knew he had somehow got tangled with another woman, and she had been very upset and mad about it for sometime. But when the woman started to call and make trouble that was it. She had to protect her husband and her family. It wasn't long before she realized she was dealing with a psycho on the other end of the line. She remembered Frank coming to her with flowers, candy, and blubbering. How could she not forgive a big teddy bear like him? She guessed he was sowing his wild oats, and after that, he had settled down and was an attentive and loving husband to her and the kids.

Frank could see that his wife was agitated and squeezed her hand to reassure her. "It'll be fine, dear. The most important thing is I have most of the gear that will help me reach town. Besides, look on the bright side. The next time you see me, you'll be looking at a new man, twenty lbs. lighter, and an experienced mountaineer." Frank chuckled before motioning behind him at the canvas bag on the couch, and the walking stick and makeshift lance standing at the front door. He had fashioned a crude, crutch like a stick from a spruce tree limb, and then notched and tied one of the metal tent stakes to the end of another limb. "Remember what I said about the can of gas out back. Be very careful with it."

"I know, hon." Alice was careful not to show her impatience with him, but she was tired of hearing the instructions for the umpteenth time.

"You have plenty of paper, and I left a good size bundle of kindling next to the fireplace. I think you'll have enough propane for another day or two to cook whatever is left, and you can also use it for an additional heat source. The wood and kindling should be dry enough to use by then, and if it gets too smoky in here, just crack the front door."

"I'm worried about you, babe. It's going to be difficult and with the deep snow and all..." Her voice trailed off, thinking about the horrible journey ahead.

"I'll be fine, and with the weather getting warmer and the equipment, it'll be a snap." Frank wasn't so sure. Without any information, especially weather conditions, he didn't know if he was stepping into a trap. The weather on the mountain could change on a dime. After their meager breakfast, he stood and helped Alice with the dishes as he usually did.

"Hon, get going, you're burning daylight." Alice looked at her teddy bear with pride and love. They embraced in a long kiss before he gathered his gear and donned his winter outerwear. Afterward, he sat on the couch, and she helped in toeing and tying on his snowshoes. She could tell that her husband did a good job. It took him two days of trial and error with the spare tire, but after he was done, he beamed with accomplishment. The rubber shoes were about two feet long with a square back and rounded in front with rope punched through to form webbing that wound around his lower legs. He could have built lattice style snowshoes out of spruce, and they would have been lighter and probably more flexible, but the tire provided a weatherproof surface, stability from the radial steel bands and a natural curvature to help keep the snow out. It was especially difficult getting through the steel bands, and if it wasn't for a big metal punch and hammer, he wouldn't have made it. The only drawback he could see is that they were a little heavier than he liked.

Frank looped the makeshift rope sling over his right arm and onto his back, that was attached to the canvas bag. He did one last check and then stepped to the front door to collect his walking stick and lance. On a whim, he asked Alice for one of her florescent orange hair bands. He told her that it would bring him luck. Finally, he turned to his wife, and with one last kiss, he said his farewell. He stepped through the door, and she watched as he disappeared into the white wilderness. She lingered for a few moments, saying some prayers before going inside.

Frank figured he had seven hours of daylight to make haste. Having lost a good ten pounds in the last two weeks working with his hands, he felt good. The sky, was slate gray with a hint of glow from the east, it dotted with Altocumulus clouds from horizon to horizon. A soft breeze from the west ushered in the news of a coming event–a competition between snow and wind. Even though it was daylight and the weather was warmer, Frank knew the going would be rough. He pushed on. He would follow High Valley Lane to Mountain Way Road, and then make a decision whether he would go cross-country. It was about four or five miles to the junction, and he hoped that he would make it by nightfall. He just wished he had a compass.

THIRTEEN

Hunters

I t was mid-morning before the group of hunters made their final push to an outcropping near one of the peaks in the San Juan Mountains. Clyde Easton looked at Earl Garvey with his sharp brown eyes and motioned that it was time to go. Earl glanced back at the rest of the party and could tell that they were ready with impatience in their eyes. Even though Clyde was young in years, he demanded attention and respect because of his gruff demeanor and attention to detail. He was tall, powerfully built, and agile in the ways of mountain climbing and took no bull from anyone, especially when climbing in high altitude. It was rumored that he once bloodied a man to pulp while on a climbing expedition and buried him in the mountains because the person would not heed his advice and instructions. In his eyes, this was no place for theatrics. After all, they were guests up here in the high elevations, and they had better heed the elements of the host's domain, lest they become prisoners of their own fault and mistakes.

Five of them had been off grid for days, hunting Bighorns in a high, sheltered valley just below the tree line above Telluride. Jim Hazelton, the leader and the most experienced in the group flipped off his snowshoes, strapped into his 'sharky shoes', front pointing crampons and grabbed his ice pick. They had stopped to rest and changed gear in order to make the final ascent to the rocky outcrop above the valley. Jim knew the sheep were there, resting, out of reach of their predators. He was a hard-bitten man and sometimes he pushed his party to the breaking point. Big in thinking and in stature, he used his credentials as a professional hunting guide to get his way. After all, he was looking for a trophy, they all were.

Jim's son, Leroy, the youngest in the group, had only gone Bighorn hunting once before, but never this high. They had been at it for five days, and Leroy was just getting acclimated to the altitude and had trouble staying up. They should have stayed longer in Telluride, but their tags and permits were only good for two weeks, and his dad wasn't one for wasting time. The weather had been bitterly cold the last few days with the North wind constantly at them. At this elevation, the mix was more ice than snow, and even though it had warmed overnight and precipitation had lessened, it was still colder than a well digger's ass and Leroy was getting more disenchanted every mile they went. He wasn't a calloused man like his father, small in stature with darting brown eyes; he was there to appease his dad. Constantly being pushed, he was getting tired of his dad's best intentions, and in fact their relationship had grown so hostile over the last few weeks that a wedge of suspicion had now embedded itself in Leroy's mind. He just wasn't himself anymore, and he was afraid of what he might do.

Frozen tundra and rock beneath their feet, they traveled on, ever higher on treacherous ground toward one of the peaks. Clyde was now at point urging them on while Earl and Leroy were closing the rear. Daylight waning and a hard day's work nearly behind, the men were getting tired. The climb was long and brutal, and the men were seeking respite to bivouac on a prized piece of nearly level ground above them. Their plan was to rest overnight on a partially sheltered parcel below the outcropping and make their strike at dawn the next day.

Already roped together, Earl and Jim, one by one, released their safety hooks and changed position with Clyde still at lead before reattaching. Secure in the knowledge of having their weight evenly distributed, they would own the best survival rate in case of a mishap. A crevasse lay ahead, and once they got past, it was a sprint to the camping area. Ever mindful of their crampons holding ice, they picked their way up the mountain, each man left to his own thoughts. Landscape nearly vertical, the mountain reluctantly deferred its position to the men working their skill. Nearing exhaustion, the group reached the lip of the overnight haven dropping their gear and worrying later about moving to the back for more shelter.

"Dad, I still don't know why you didn't leave me below with Humberto. I'm sure you could've herded the Bighorns without me." Leroy looked at his dad in annoyance while laying on the precious catch of level land, finding his breath. "Besides, I'm a better shot than Humberto."

"You're not even close, son. Humberto Sanchez was a marksman in the Army. He not only knows rifles and handguns, he preps his own loads and is an excellent scout."

"Well, I still think I'm better," Leroy said in anger, while eyeing a spot towards the back of the catch.

His dad looked up to the outcropping and pointed. "You see that up there?'

"Sure, what's the big deal?"

"We're about 12,000 feet, and the outcropping isn't too far below the crest."

"So?" His son interrupted. He was tired and hungry, and wanted to get to the back of the pocket for some food and rest.

Jim looked at his son again in amazement, his deep brown eyes snapping. "I need four up here to make sure the sheep don't break to the peak and go over the other side. If so, we can kiss off the last few days of hard work. Bert will be ready when they enter the valley." Without saying more, Jim collected his gear and headed to the back. It was dusk now, and they had precious few hours to rest and prepare for tomorrow. His son grudgingly trudged behind his father. Earl and Clyde, shaking their heads, looked on as they brought up the rear. Trouble was brewing as surly as dusk was marching toward dawn.

FOURTEEN

High Valley Lane

It was early afternoon, and Frank reckoned that he was a mile or so from the junction. He stopped a ways back to have some trail mix and apple slices from one of the sandwich baggies that Alice had packed and washed it down with a handful of snow. Would have been nice to add some vanilla and have a flavored snow cone–he could only wish. His plan was to eat half a sandwich each morning and evening, and trail mix and fruit during the day to sustain his energy. He only had three sandwiches made from stale bread. After that, it was leftover trail mix and sheer will power to the finish. He was getting tired, but feeling good as he walked on. The snow markers kept him on track, and snow wasn't as deep here. His makeshift snowshoes were holding up, though, he had to stop every few hundred feet and clean the wells with his lance, because the snow buildup made them heavier. He probably should have taken the extra time and care and made lattice style snowshoes out of spruce, but didn't want to miss his window of opportunity in case the weather broke. He just hoped this would not be his undoing.

Weather agreeing with a constant slate gray sky and only an occasional rift of snow, he was making good progress. Having stopped again to mop his heavy brow, he had taken his coat off and cursed himself for being in such poor shape. If they get through this, he promised himself that he and Alice would change their ways and exercise from here on out. *What was he thinking, taking her here?* His brown eyes scanned the horizon for heavy snow clouds; there weren't any. Good. He was concerned about the mountain lion tracks he spotted a mile back. It was three sets. *Probably a mother and her cubs,* he thought, as he gripped the lance tighter and checked for his hunting knife. Frank wondered if she was the one screaming last night or on Christmas night. He would have to keep a sharp eye out.

As he came around a long bend in the road, he could just make out the junction to Mountain Way Road off in the distance. It was hazy and nearly dusk. As he stopped again to rest and adjust his backpack, something caught his attention above and to the right of him. He spun around to get a better look and spotted movement one hundred yards out. It was gray and moving fast toward him. Whipping off his snow goggles and peering through the gloom, he could now see that it was a huge gray wolf closing ranks. He reached down to collect his hunting knife from the scabbard and pointed his lance towards the direction of the wolf. A chill ran through his bones as he realized that he was in mortal danger. Thank God he saw it when he did, otherwise, he would've been blind-sided.

Rollo had been tracking its prey for the last hour or so, gauging his quickness and agility. It didn't seem threatening, and in fact was slow and clumsy. The thing would stop every once in a while to check something on his feet. He waited until the road's snow bank gave sufficient cover before he made his move. He couldn't hold his hunger at bay much longer and only hoped that he would find the right terrain to launch from. As he got closer to his target, the familiar scent of fear and uncertainty overwhelmed his senses. He knew these things were dangerous, but his hunger was now overpowering, and besides, he found that he enjoyed the killings after the splitting. He wasn't even sure if he would share his kill with the others this time. He was tired of their rejections and rudeness. Even though he knew he was different since the incident, he also knew that some of the change came from the way he was treated. As he got closer, he could see the figure was now facing him and holding something in his hand. He didn't care.

With wild abandon, the huge gray creature bunched his muscles and sprang off the snow bank toward his prey.

FIFTEEN

The Attack

R ocketing over the snow bank like a shell exploding from a cannon, the wolf was on its prey in an instant. Frank couldn't believe the ferocity and the speed of the attack. With his serrated knife already drawn and lance at hand he, thought he was ready–he wasn't. He spun just in time as the wolf hit his backpack and they tumbled in the snow. Gaining leverage from his lance he sprung upright and slashed at the wolf's forehead as the creature came at him again. The carnivore yelped as he went by. Frank knew he hit pay dirt because this momentarily slowed the assault and gave him time to maneuver the lance in the wolf's direction.

Bleeding profusely from one of his eyes, Rollo's vision was clouded as he sized up his opponent. He was leery, but hunger and meanness drove him on. He circled his adversary, looking for an opening. Even though his prey was larger than himself, he was fearless. Circling again to get closer, Rollo jabbed and weaved in order to throw his assailant off balance. The deadly game continued. At times, the canine was the aggressor; other times, it was his foe. Rollo was surprised at how quick his enemy reacted to his moves. As the encounter went on, Rollo was growing impatient and yet more wary of his rival. Surly, the thing would tire and afford him an opening before long. He kept eying the instrument in his prey's hand. It was long, and pointed, and portended to more pain if he wasn't careful. His forehead and eye painful as it was, kept him alert and reminded him of the perils in dealing with this kind. Just then, the figure threw something out at him and it, and landed nearby. Rollo's senses were assaulted with the sharp smell of meat.

The distraction was just enough for Frank to get near enough and drive the metal tent stake deep into the wolf's side. The creature let out a long wail of pain as he drove the stake deeper. All of sudden Frank felt the bone crushing pressure on his arm, holding the lance, from the wolf's jaws. The force was so intense that it nearly broke his forearm. The material from his coat and shirt melted away as the wolf tore at him. It wasn't long before he could feel the creature's canines and incisors shred his arm, and feel the pain, and see his blood exploding to the snow in images of crimson red. With his other hand, he wildly swung the knife at the carnivore, hitting him in his back and along his flanks. They were now locked in a battle of death, rolling in the snow and turning it red wherever they had been.

Just then, off in the distance, they heard a howling that was of another world. As it grew closer, the wolf released his hold on him and looked behind. This was enough for Frank to slide away from his adversary. As he continued to make distance from the wolf, he saw and heard a strange, haunting vision behind the wolf. His mind couldn't comprehend what his eyes were seeing. All of a sudden, in the gloom, he saw fleeting images of a needle-like outline of a huge gray wolf come out of nowhere. It was as if he was seeing tracer bullets arcing across the horizon in staccato-like fashion. *What was it?* He thought. The apparition was so unnerving that he momentarily forgot about the pain in his arm. The huge silver-gray figure was now standing in front of his aggressor in the snow with silver-like saliva dripping from its jaws. Frank remained perfectly still afraid to move as he took in the scene. The wolf on the ground looked up at the ghost-like figure; Frank could clearly see that there was fear in the wolf's eyes. What riveted Frank's attention the most was that they both had blue eyes. He didn't notice his adversary's eyes before, but now he could see that they were a dark blue, while the others were sky-blue.

Rollo was terrified, looking at the apparition in front of him.

What was he trying to tell him? His instincts told him to be careful. He hated the power that the ghost-like wolf had over him. He still wasn't sure what had happened when the bear attacked him only that he was different now. Afterward, he knew that his "other" was not only close by, but also always seemed to be stalking him, always keeping an eye on him. It was always interfering with his kills, and somehow he knew there would be a reckoning. He bared his fangs and snarled at the phantom-like creature. The entity only looked at him with boredom in his sky- blue eyes. The battle with the human was now long forgotten as he tried to break the hypnotic trance that the creature had on him. Eventually, he was able to look away and attend to his wounds.

The specter sensing that his friend was now out of danger withdrew and vanished in the gloom, leaving behind wolf tracks that disappeared in the snow. With all the fight taken out of him, Rollo hobbled away.

Frank sat in the snow, thinking about what he had just seen.

Looking in the direction of the wolf prints, they disappeared in the snow a few feet out from where they had started. *How could this be? How could any of this be?* He thought. Was it the wolf that he and Alice saw when driving to the cabin? By now, the wolf and the apparition were long gone, but the tattered pieces of the scene, disjointed, remained in his mind. He couldn't put it together, at least not yet, but he knew he had seen something, and that something disturbed him very much. *Was he losing it?* He looked down, the sight of his blood, and the pain shooting through his arm told him differently–there was something, and it was real. He needed to gather his thoughts and concentrate on wrapping his forearm to stem the bleeding. He took off his coat and used his knife to cut some of the coat's interior lining into strips to bind his arm. He needed a sling, but there wasn't enough cloth, so he had to make do. It was nearly dark, and he still had a half mile to the junction. He managed to slip his good arm into his coat. He was weak and getting cold, and lamented about wasting half a sandwich, but in all likelihood, it probably saved his life, and he was grateful for that.

After arriving at the junction, Frank surveyed the road in both directions and saw there had been no recent activity as far as cars or snowplows. In the last hour or so it had cleared, and he could see a Wolf Moon rising from the east that offered a double- edged set of circumstances. One side indicated a cold night ahead, clear without snow, while the other offered no hope of a snowplow. Frank pulled his coat tighter, around him, to ward off the evening chill. He now remembered about the visquene he was carrying and he dug it out of his backpack and cut some of it in strips for a sling. With great difficulty, he managed to tie a couple of strips together and looped it around him. Afterward he scrounged for dry twigs and branches. Finding some and using his knife with his good arm, he shaved kindling and shoveled a small snow enclosure with his good hand and his lance. With a small fire going, he rolled out the rest of the visquene, sat on it, and changed his chemical packs. The old ones were spent, and his hands and feet were getting cold again. Eating a stale half sandwich, he thought about what century he was in and hoped Alice was fine.

He knew he was vulnerable out here in the wilderness, especially without communications, information, and newer winter technology, but he would have to make do. The wolf attack had surprised him, and he only hoped that he could make it to Telluride and get help for Alice. The pain was still throbbing, and interfering with his thinking, so he delayed his decision until tomorrow morning whether, to go cross-country or try the road. Perhaps after getting some rest, his thinking would become clearer. Best thing now was to calm down, keep his lance, and hunting knife nearby and try and get some sleep. *Good luck*, he thought.

SIXTEEN

Sheepherding

Night came with no fire. Granola bars, apples, and bananas made their rounds. The next morning, after tidying up, the four men paired up and moved laterally and quietly along the slope below the outcropping. Their plan was for each pair of men to circumvent the herd and come up behind them before discharging their long arms. If successful, the herd would bolt and be driven to the valley below, where Humberto was waiting for them.

"Dad, how come I'm always paired with you?" Leroy asked.

"Well, son, if you're going to shoot somebody, it might as well be me."

Anger flashed in Leroy's brown eyes. "You know dad, I'm getting tired of your stupid, fatalist humor. If you can't say anything sensible, then don't say anything at all."

"Pipe down and keep your voice low. I know you're a good shot. I want you with me to show you how I approach and corral the sheep. There is a method to my madness, and it generally works. Besides, it's good working with you. Now hush up, it's stealth time."

Leroy just looked at his dad and kept his thoughts to himself. As usual, he knew his dad was right and knew that he was a good hunter. Most of the year, his father was a professional guide and led hunts in

Canada and the northern U.S. for a variety of game, but his specialty was Bighorn.

As the men flanked the herd from the east and west ends of the ledge, Jim could see that the lambs were resting between the upper and lower outcropping from the west end. There were four of them. He couldn't see the rams or ewes, but he knew they were there, probably just out of eyesight. The ground nearly vertical and slick with ice, the group was using the outer facing of the higher outcropping for additional leverage. As the men crept along the backset of rocks near the ridge, one of the rams stood and scented the air. Everyone froze, stayed low, and listened. The air, cold with frost signaled hardly a breeze. *Good,* Jim thought. *Didn't want them to pick up his scent.* At this elevation, air ringing with silence, sound traveled as far as one could see and sometimes beyond.

Aware of steel grating against stone, the men continued on. As everyone neared their positions, the mob became restless, shifting about, listening, and scenting the air. Jim glanced back to see if Leroy was properly spaced, he was. *Almost there,* he thought. *Just a few more steps until he would hear the sharp crack of rifles in the air.*

Then it happened. Leroy lost his footing and slipped over the second outcropping, sliding toward the first line of rocks as Jim reached for the nearest stratum. Sounds reverberated in the chilled air mixed with the clatter of hooves, screaming, and discharging firearms as the herd bolted down the mountain slope to the valley below. Rocks clawing at Jim's hands, he could feel the violent pull of his son's weight descending on his climber's harness like a person drawn between two horses. Quickly, Clyde and Earl worked their way over to Jim in crablike fashion. Clyde grabbed Leroy's safety line to ease the pressure on Jim and braced his feet against the outcropping while Earl scampered down the ice to reach Leroy. Clyde strained to hold both climbers until Jim recovered and was able to get a better hold on his son's lifeline.

Looking up, Leroy could hear Earl asking if he was okay. Embarrassment just a shy away, he answered, "Yeah, I'm fine."

Reaching Leroy, Earl helped the younger man to the lower outcropping. Giving Leroy the once-over, he could tell that his pride was hurt more than his bones. "What happened?"

"Had my hand on the wrong side of the rocks, and when my weight shifted to move further up line I slipped and couldn't recover in time with my other hand." Sheepishly, Leroy looked up at Earl and knew what was coming next.

"How long you've been climbing?" "Long enough."

Earl reached over to help Leroy up. "You know I shouldn't have to tell you this, but what were you thinking. You always have a hand on rock if you can when traversing icy slopes. It's like tree walking–always have a safety line attached–especially when moving around trees."

"How's my dad taking it?"

"Well, you'll have to ask him yourself. I'm sure he is concerned about your wellbeing as we all are, but seeing that you're in one piece; you may not be for long. Jim saved your bacon, son."

Earl turned as Clyde and Jim approached, and motioned Clyde aside so, Jim and his son could be alone. "I'm sure they have a few things to discuss," Earl said.

"I wouldn't want to be in Leroy's shoes right about now." Clyde collected another plug of chew and placed it in his lower right cheek. "I don't know if he'll be coming on our next hunt. He's making too many mistakes, and I think his dad is getting tired of baby-sitting him."

Earl adjusted his stance on the icy slope and looked sideways at his friend. "I don't know why Jim allowed him to come along in the first place. We all know that Leroy isn't interested in mountain climbing, let alone bighorn hunting. I think Jim is just trying to build some character in his son."

Clyde shot a stream of snooze across the ice and snow. The contrast was amazing, and it almost looked like blood but without the coppery smell. "Well, I think that's a dangerous way of building character, and I'm sure as hell wouldn't want to be in Leroy's shoes."

Everyone looked up as they heard the crack of a high- powered rifle break the silence, echoing across the mountainside. Clyde and Earl made their way down to where Jim and Leroy were standing.

"Well, let's go and see what Bert bagged for us," Jim said.

As the four started to make their way down the mountainside between patches of ice and tundra, two more shots ringed from the valley below. While picking their way down, Jim was thinking how much the Rockies had changed in the last 150 years. He could even see it himself since climbing the mountains as a kid. Much of the glaciers had receded in the past 150 years in the Rockies that made mountain climbing less technical in some places, but more dangerous in others. He wasn't sure if it was due to man or the cycles of the sun, but he did know change was here.

SEVENTEEN

Another Decision

Frank awoke early the next morning to silence. He had trouble sleeping because of his arm and thinking about Alice.

Something more was bothering him: a wolf had entered his dreams, or had it been here with him in the snow cave–he couldn't tell. It had troubled and awakened him several times during the night. Huge with sky blue eyes, it didn't seem threatening–a benign presence looking after him. *Was it the same creature that tried to protect him during the wolf attack or the one he saw on the road?* It seemed so real that he could almost reach out and touch it. He wondered why he had dreamt this. *Did it mean something?* It just kept looking at him as if to tell him something. Peering through a cloud of gray, looking at him in a quizzical manner, moving its massive head side to side, and its sky blue eyes radiating out of the darkness, Frank felt it wanted something, but what? He didn't know what to make of it. He did recall as a child that he had been a lucid dreamer, often remembering in great detail what his dreams were about. Sometimes he would walk to his dream vault, where his dreams were stored, and choose which dream he would dream next. There were other times, though, when he would wake, mad, furious of not remembering the code to the vault. *Was this one of those times?* He thought. Other times he had recalled having reoccurring dreams of a huge gray wolf slinking outside the vault not letting him in–was this the same creature–he wasn't sure.

He attended to his arm before pulling back the visquene with his good hand to see another day of slate gray skies. The temperature seemed to be holding steady with very little wind. He checked the floor of his small enclosure for paw prints–there were none. *Strange,* he thought, *it seemed so real.* Reaching in his bag for a stale half sandwich, he was thinking on which direction to travel. Should he continue trekking the road or head cross- country? He had already covered five miles to the junction yesterday, and by staying on the road, he had about seventeen miles to go. Best estimates gave him twelve miles with a direct route heading due south to Telluride. He was a gambler, but not with his life. Mountain Way Road, it would be.

He tied on his snowshoes as best he could and gathered his gear. It was time to do another five or six miles. Even though he was tired from the attack and his arm sore, he was in a good mood the weather was holding, and the road ahead was packed snow and ice because it was more traveled than the road to their cabin. Maybe he would see someone driving the road. He could only hope. As he traveled down the route, something loomed in front of him. Large and white, the road seemed to disappear into it.

Christ! He thought. *It's 's a snow slide.* He hadn't been aware of any avalanche danger–no information about this in town. *Must have recently happened,* he thought. With no communication and hardly anything modern, he was stuck. Instincts were his best friend, and he just hoped with what little winter training he had at Mt.

Washington, it would be enough. Approaching the slide, he could see a snarled mass of trees sprouting from its top and the side of it was like a box of disarranged wooden matchsticks. Peering closer, he could see car-sized boulders and chunks of ice scattered around and in the slide field. Mixed with mud and earth gave the morass an ugly appearance akin to a train of debris. Frank's brown eyes knitted with amazement. Looking both ways, the avalanche extended as far as one could see. *It was at least one hundred feet high and lord knows how wide,* he thought.

He walked to the edge of the debris field, extended his lance and poked around. The snow was soft in places but hard in others. *What could've caused this?* Sitting on one of the smaller boulders and munching trail mix, he pondered his next move. He had made only a mile or so and knew this was going to cause a delay. *How much?* This was massive. *Was there an earthquake?* He and Alice hadn't felt anything. It certainly wasn't spring snow where conditions sometimes grow unstable and layers of snow would rumble down the mountainside. This was deeper reinforced by the sight of huge boulders and trees. Well, it looked like the decision was made for him—he would now go cross-country and hope for the best. Perhaps he only needed to go a mile or so and then double back to the road.

Frank looked around again and spotted tracks coming off the avalanche and heading north up the mountain. He knelt and peered at them closely. They were broad, over four inches across with four evenly spaced toe prints. Its rear of the heel pad had three lobes. Deep in the snow, they signified a large male cat—over two hundred pounds, he guessed. And the cat was heading in the general direction of the cabin. He hoped that Alice was okay and was now torn between heading back or pushing on. *Surly, the cougar couldn't get in.* He glanced up to check the weather. It seemed colder, and there were now snow clouds on the horizon. He leveraged the walking stick with his good arm, climbed up, and over the plow's snow bank and headed south toward Telluride.

The snow, much deeper, created difficulty, and his breathing labored as he pushed on.

Cabin

I t was changing. Peering through one of the small windows in the cabin, Alice could feel it. Wiping rime off the inside of the panes she could see the stunted trees around the property, noise in their branches, waving to her, watching over the land. The wind's infernal howling had subsided and then quit altogether the night before Frank had left, but now the cycle was renewing itself. She was worried about him. It had been over two days and she hoped that he was making good progress because the weather looked threatening. She figured her husband was just shy of half way to Telluride and hoped he was okay. In the last couple of weeks she had seen a change in him. He seemed more fit and confident about his ways. Maybe chopping wood and shoveling snow was really what they needed. The mornings had been the worst, waking alone to another day of fretting, running the tread mill of life, wondering if she would die far from her loved ones, frozen, tucked away in the mountains.

Yesterday was calm, but now it was growing colder, with the wind rising. She supposed it wouldn't be long before the snow followed. She looked around the sparse cabin and wrung her hands. There were just so many hands of solitaire one could play. The food supply was down to broth, pieces of stale bread, and a few potatoes, and the fuel wasn't much better. It was time to stoke the fire, but this time she needed gasoline to keep the fire going.

The wood she had brought in yesterday was still wet, with little paper, she had no choice. She followed her husband's instructions and was careful with the petrol–just a little at a time until the wood caught. Afterward, she went to the kitchen to reuse one of her tea bags. It wasn't much, but it least it was something.

She looked around at the remodeled kitchen and thought what a wonderful job her husband did. It was nice and warm, and cozy, and she particularly liked the stone counters that were installed. She hugged the shirt around her to ward off the cold.

The winter chill rushed headlong into the night as silver dots beckoned from above and draped themselves over the frozen landscape.

Alice worried about the tracks she had seen out front. They were large, and she wondered if it was a wolf or a cougar. *Maybe it was the wolf she saw on the road.* Either way, they were menacing and could bring trouble–more trouble than she was already in. This morning, when she had looked outside, there were more. She had remembered going to the kitchen and retrieving a large kitchen knife before exploring around the back. She had found that the snow was disturbed by a group of prints below one of the windows. *Was something looking in?* She hadn't recalled hearing anything during the night–no screaming or anything like what she and Frank had heard the day before he left. *Were there tracks then?* She didn't know; Frank didn't say anything.

She thought about weapons; she was unarmed except for some kitchen knives, a splitting maul, a double-bladed ax, and a firewood poker. She went outside to retrieve the ax; she wanted more protection in case she needed it. A cold sweat broke over her–a fear of the unknown.

It was now late afternoon, and snow was falling again. Alice peered out at the thermometer and saw that it had fallen ten degrees since morning. *Fine vacation*, she thought. She was now thinking about her husband again, with the snow falling and temperature dropping, she was worried about him. It was a long way to Telluride, especially in these conditions, and she prayed that Frank would make it. She hoped he was okay and making good progress for both of their sake. *She loved him more than he would ever know*, she thought. Tears trickled from the corners of her blue eyes.

It was time for dinner. She needed to go through the motions of preparing a regular meal. It would help calm her nerves. *She walked to the alcove, but what was she going to cook?* At best she had two days before she was down to melted snow. *She wondered what it was like to starve to death; she may find out,* she thought. After a fine meal of potato soup, she stoked the fire and added another couple of small logs. The cabin was getting smoky again from the damp wood, so she propped open the door for ventilation since the windows wouldn't open, they were painted shut. She could either breathe and freeze or stay warm and suffocate–some choice, that was. Mostly, she was terrified of wild animals coming through the door. As darkness slid deeper into the night, she thought she heard some scratching on the front porch. Collecting her ax, she went to investigate. Finding nothing and turning, she was just inside the door and was about to close it when something caught her attention from the corner of her eye. Alice instinctively ducked. She knew it was big as it flew past her, knocking her to the floor.

NINETEEN

Sanchez

Humberto dragged the log close to a stand of stunted spruce. He wanted one end just past the clump of trees pointing east, next to a hollow of ground. Perfect for his rest. He could crouch here without being seen, and it would afford an excellent view to the valley's upper end, and hopefully this is where the band of rams would come through. The herd had already been sheltering from the tough winter conditions before the men had arrived. Humberto and Jim had spotted them from the air early last summer and had set up cameras to get an idea of the herd size, their grazing habits, travel patterns, and how many prized rams where in the group. Thinking back, they had already applied for their tags and licenses through the Colorado Parks and Wildlife lottery and had the phenomenal luck of garnering two tags for bighorn rams last spring. No one in the group had the money to apply and bid in the state's special lottery–only wealth wins there. The bighorn population in the western part of the country had dwindled to about 17,000 by the seventies. When some of the states instituted a lottery system in the late seventies, grumblings were heard throughout the hunting community. Next, came the specialized auctions, and together they were used for the conservation and management of the species. He knew that there were over 75,000 now and growing. Even though they had to play by the rules and were only permitted to grid hunt the payoffs could be huge.

Humberto looked north to the valley entrance. All was quiet. It had been decided yesterday that the valley was too wide and open for the five hunters to flank them, so it was better to track them to the high ridges, corral them, and turn them for the run back into the valley. Heavily scented in ewe musk, the lone hunter crouched in the hollow, next to the log, waiting for his targets. The only thing new about the 300 Weatherby magnum he was using was the scope. He was one of the few that had been asked to test the new equipment, from an Israeli company, because of his renowned sharp shooting experience in the military. The new Laser Identification, Detection, and Ranging (LIDAR) scopes are not only measured elevation and wind age, such as wind vectors to gauge wind velocity and direction, but also used a rangefinder laser technology for target distance. He also knew that the LIDAR scope included a weather package for humidity and barometric pressure. Sanchez was anxious to try out the new scope on live targets, and as far as riffles, he still liked the older 300 Weatherby. Reliable, was the word that came to mind. Bolt action, long range and flat trajectory were the ticket for this outing. He had been using the rifle for years with various grain loads, and it hadn't failed him yet. Although he was worried about the wind since it had kicked up from the north, and being downwind could be iffy. *Hope the musk holds*, he thought. What took his friends a good half-day to reach the high ridges above the valley only took the rams less than an hour to reach the opening. *It wouldn't be long now.*

As the lead ram broke into the upper end of the valley, Humberto scoped him, and he could see he was a beauty. Well over two hundred pounds with a magnificent rack, he looked young and was in good shape. The rest of the herd followed and he could see four more rams. He already knew the count, and makeup of the herd from the pictures the cameras had taken in the last few months. In some ways, he felt sad that technology eliminated most of the surprises and guesswork. It was almost mechanical now. In the rush for more knowledge, they forgot that they had lost some of the excitement and felt almost boring at times. And now there was talk of smart bullets coming from the military. *What was next?*

The tags were for Jim and himself. Clyde, Earl, and Leroy would get their shot next year. The two would draw straws to determine the outcome of the kill or kills, including the size of the racks. He checked the read outs on the bottom of the scope. The big fella was within 300 yards and closing. The heart shot ricocheted across the valley as Humberto scoped for the next one. He had to be quick, lest his chances be squandered. The herd was already turning as two more shots rang out. He extracted the three shot magazine and slammed home another. He didn't need to.

The second one was down and bleeding in the snow. Away from the sound, the herd bolted up the mountain. Humberto didn't care. Short in disposition and stature, he was a solitary man, resolute in his ways, his nearly black eyes reflected as much. He slung the rifle over his shoulder and headed toward the two rams, now lying still in the snow. His companions were at least a couple of hours out, and this would give him a good start on removing the heads. He had to be careful, though, because they would be mounted on trophy plaques. He didn't mind the extra effort, and in fact, he enjoyed the precision. They had already made arrangements for the carcasses and the helo would be here at first light in the morning.

TWENTY

The Other

Huge and menacing, the creature had been tracking the hiker in deep snow for over an hour. Its sky blue eyes leveled to the lone figure, deciding the fate of its prey. Scenting told him there was no fear, and that made the doppelganger apprehensive. Normally, he wouldn't be tracking this scent. But what was the quarry? Foreign in familiarity made him even more cautious.

Studying intently, he kept his distance from the slow moving target, gauging his senses. Now on, top of the snow pile, he looked down at the figure. Struggling, it seemed too busy to be aware of him. Always stopping, always scraping the being moved on, following the slide using a long pole. He was sorry that he hadn't arrived sooner to fend off the attack, but he at least chased his "other" away. He wondered if he should call the others like he had in the past. He knew they were hungry, always searching, especially in winter, but something going against instinct told him otherwise. He was here to help, possibly to redeem his spirit.

The hunger and passion had never left him since the splitting eight months ago. The incident had left him feeling bewildered, angry, and confused, yet giving. *Was he alone, or were there others like him? What had he become?* He often thought of that frightful day, caught in two different worlds, clawing for ownership and never realizing purchase in either one. Dreams tormenting, he anguished seeing deceptions within illusions, the "other goer" crawling away from the fight of his life, severely wounded and bleeding, lying in the creek bed. *What was he fighting? Was he fighting himself, the "other goer"? And if so, why?* He hadn't ever recalled attacking the other creature, lying helpless staring up at him. He had just been born of spirit, tempered, and melded with the god of fire and water–Vulcan and Neptune. But they were fighting something, or rather, the "other goer", was fighting something. Maybe that something was what drove him to being what he was today. It seemed so long ago, and now it was becoming a part of him, always reminding him of the transformation. More than a set of circumstances, a flash point leading him to this place. He had sensed the agony that he went through perhaps for days just trying to survive, the pain so intense that it struck to the very core of his being. And then there was the heat, the shearing heat that enveloped him while he was changing.

He had only remembered coming to, standing over the "other goer" in ice-cold water, nearly changed. After bounding to the creek's bank, he had remembered that the violence of the ordeal melded into a sensation of wellbeing and benevolence.

Everywhere he went, he was always trying to help his brethren, looking out for others. He couldn't remember if he was part of a family group, but if he continued to search, he was sure that he would find something. He agonized to become that something or so he thought.

He had felt better than he had ever in his life, bigger and stronger than before. But was there a before, he wasn't sure. Wise in his ways and instincts, acute in all manners, he could see farther and hear well beyond the range of normal wolves. Sight reached and sound traveled almost unrestrained in his new domain–trees, mountains, animals and even creeks and rivers gained new perspective. The ground he traveled held a certain fluorescents and trees, and all things where iridescent in nature. He could almost feel his environment–everything around him seemed alive.

He had been bothered, though. Whenever he reached out for his kind they always treated him with suspicion, confusion, and fear. Even though he probably wasn't a member of the packs, he encountered, he never remembered being rebuffed so rudely. It was indifference at best and sometimes hostile and coldness that led to violence more than naught. He didn't want it this way. He always won because he was larger, stronger, and faster than the others. He wasn't sure if they could see him, perhaps glimpses here and there, but he knew they could sense him. Sometimes he would kill his own to strike fear in them. Other times, he would bring down game and signal his brethren to the kill zone, and stand back and watch them feast from a distance.

He had remembered, not too long ago, finding his family. They didn't know him anymore, and this saddened him. It hadn't even been eight months–he was surprised. Nonetheless, like others he had done before, he went off and provided a kill. One time after bringing down a coyote, he signaled for his pack, but his howl was mixed with another noise he hadn't heard before. Was it his kind? He had waited a long time and was about to leave when his family finally arrived. He had tried to greet his mate for life as the pack approached the kill, but she ignored his presence.

Somehow he had known that she sensed that he was different and couldn't understand why. He was excited to tell her and the others what he had gone through and what he had learned from the experience, but they weren't interested. He wondered why his "other" was never around when he was near the pack. Perhaps there were boundaries, after all, and he couldn't be at the same place at the same time with him. He would find out. One thing for certain, no matter what he had tried, be it kindness, goodwill, or friendship, he was always met with rejection. He wasn't sure if it was he or the pack, but over the last eight months, his outlook had changed toward them from longing to anger, and he knew the relationship would never be the same.

The doppelganger climbed a huge boulder in the snow pile to get a better view of the lone intruder. The thing had stopped again, and was pulling something out of its pocket. The smell, sharp, sliced through the air, assaulting the creature's senses. *What was it?* He wasn't sure. But now, perched on the rock with his ears pointed forward he, knew he had to help the intrepid intruder because it was showing no fear. Jaws slacked, eyes concentrating, he bounded off the rock and surged ahead, coming off the slope three hundred feet in front of the lone figure, and was gone.

TWENTY-ONE

South

Wondering if he had made a mistake, Frank trudged on in deep snow, one hundred feet out, and parallel to the avalanche. Even though it had grown smaller, he could see no end in sight and his progress had been slow. He had stopped a while ago to rest and take some nourishment. The trail mix was damp and becoming depleted, as was his energy. He had been at it for three hours and reckoned he made a mile or so for his efforts. At this rate, it would take him forever to get to Telluride. He was hampered by snow build up on his makeshift snowshoes, always stopping to remove it in order to reduce the weight. He should have made snowshoes out of spruce saplings instead of a spare tire. *What a bonehead move,* he thought.

He had noticed tracks coming off the snow slide a way back and wondered what they were. Three and a half inches across, they were too large for a wolf, but the toe prints were too narrow to be a cougar. *It had to be a wolf–one helluva wolf,* but he couldn't figure out why the prints were so shallow lying in the snow and yet so large–it didn't make sense. And then there was the mystery of the tracks disappearing in thin air. They just stopped–nothing. *Strange.* He thought.

Another hour went by, and still he plodded on. The snow slide finally ended, and off in the distance, he could see a white, level expanse. He was too far to turn back and skirt the avalanche to Mountain Way

Road, so he continued. *A lake,* he thought. He remembered seeing a frozen lake just before the junction to Mountain Way Road. He'd been checking some of the trees along the way to make sure he was heading south. This confirmed it. He knew the main road was east of him and near the lake. The weather had turned colder, and snow had been falling lightly for the last hour. As he neared the body of frozen water, Frank could see tracks in front of him. They appeared out of nowhere. *How odd.* Kneeling, he examined the prints in the snow and found that he was looking at the exact same tracks that he had seen earlier.

There was the same indentation below the heal pad on the right forepaw. It looked like a scar. The prints were leading out onto the lake. Frank stopped at the edge and looked to the horizon in front of him. It was difficult to tell where the lake left off and the sky began. Testing the ice at the edge with his walking stick, he wondered if he should attempt to cross. The lake was larger than he remembered. Brown eyes scanning the expanse, he followed the tracks. They went out about one hundred and fifty feet, turned and came back to shore. *What was this all about?* He thought. *What's making the tracks? How come they suddenly appear and disappear? And how can the tracks be so shallow with such a large paw print?* He knew the answers wouldn't come easy; in fact, they may not come at all.

He'd been at it for nearly two days, alone, in the white wilderness. Perhaps he had lost his sense of propriety, traveling down the street of delusions, seeing things blowing by, riding the winds of illusion. He didn't know. He only knew the tracks came back to shore, and that meant something. He was now thinking on the primal level; more instinct than thought. His gut told him what to do. Told him not to go out onto the frozen lake, for if he did, he may never reach the other side. There were too many hazards out there. He may get caught in a white out and lose his way, fall through the ice or a hundred other mishaps, imagined or unimagined. No, he would head due east and find the main road and take it to Telluride.

Frank slogged on. He found that he could make better time on some of the steeper inclines by pushing off and using his walking stick with his good arm to help balance him while sliding down the slopes. He was hungry, constantly thinking of food. But discipline was the key. He only had one stale ham and rye sandwich left, and he promised himself that he would wait until he reached the main road before dining. He figured he would rest there for the night and move on the next day. As he crested another hill, he peered off into the distance. *Was that the main road up ahead?* He removed his cap and mopped his heavy brow before looking down. Studying, he could see that the slope was steep and long. *Should he chance it, especially with his bad arm?* He put his cap back on and pushed off. It wasn't long before he was riding the slope like a skier, freewheeling down the hill, looking for adventure. Surprisingly, he felt good, must be the adrenaline and the site of the main road. Before long he, was blistering down the slope, at least for him, using his walking stick for balance. Going too fast, he tried slowing by dragging his stick behind him. His lance was useless because of his damaged arm. Up ahead, at the edges of the shadows, fear rolled across his mind, seeing the jagged white maw of a crevasse. His left arm strained to leverage the walking utensil, dragging behind him in the snow. He was slowing, but was it enough. As he rolled to get more leverage, his stick dug into the snow, flipping him sideways and then on his back. Losing his walking stick, he catapulted into the jaws of the crevasse.

TWENTY-TWO

Adversary

The big male cat slammed against the back wall of the cabin, snarling. Mad as hell, misjudging its prey, it tried to turn, but was ensnared in something large. Rising, half paralyzed, fear pushing her on, Alice had only a moment or two to get to safety–to get to the bathroom. Outside, she would freeze to death. She rolled, using the ax handle as leverage to get closer to safety. Panic welling in her blue eyes; she lunged, praying she would make it. *A couple of steps away,* she thought. It wasn't far, but space and time were now a premium as the cougar clawed and kicked the couch aside to get at her. The couch had flipped, momentarily pinning the big cat against the back wall after hitting one end and crashing to the far side. The cougar bunched and sprang. Gaining time, Alice kicked the table in front of it, going through and slamming the door shut just as the cat smashed against it. Locking it, the bathroom walls shook with the force of a freight train as the big cat crashed against the door again. She knew it might not hold–she needed something. She was holding it. She jammed the broad, flat edge of the ax handle under the doorknob and kicked and stomped the bottom of the blade into the floor. It would have to do. She looked around, the small space; anything would help.

Tearing the towel fixture from the wall, beveled on each end, she was holding a double-ended spear. Not much, but it might be the difference between life and death.

The silver devil screamed, frustrated in its attempt to get at its prey. Big and powerful, the male cat circled the room, clawing, kicking, looking for anything to attack. It wailed again, and then moved to the bedroom, stopped, scenting the air for prey, for anything–it was mad. Its eyes, windows to the fires of hell, searched the room. Finding nothing, it shredded the bed, mattress in all, showing its disdain. Padding back into the cabin's main room it lunged at the bathroom door again, sinking its huge hindquarters into the floor for leverage and grinding its fore claws into the door's wood frame. Twisting at the structure, it growled deeply trying to throw fear into its victim. Impatient for food it cried again, anguishing in its hunger.

Sounds drifting in through the opened front door, the mountain devil backed away, its instincts telling of another enemy. Moving to the cabin's front entry, its sandy- green eyes peered into the darkness. The cat stepped to the front porch, scenting the air. Trickling through was the same scent that was in the cabin.

Were there others? The big cat padded around the cabin in the deep snow exploring, searching, its fur hackling as confusion competed with instinct. His head, huge, swung around, eyes narrowing as it peered into a pair of sky-blue eyes off in the distance. Scenting again, fear replaced hunger as the big cat screamed. *What was it?* Blinking, the eyes moved in distance and time. They were now much closer, more pronounced, as if the cat was sensing derealization. Menacing in sight, a huge gray figure took shape out of the evening gloom, shoulders hunched, shadows of death emerging ever closer. The mountain devil shrieked again as it leapt onto the cabin's roof, backing to the crown, bristling with fear. With jaws agape, canines gleaming, those fiery blue eyes came at the cat. In an instant, its gaze drilled into the cat's consciousness, filling its vision with terror. Glancing off the mountain lion, the apparition was gone as quickly as it came. On the roof, the silver devil swung around and peered into the darkness, staring, trying to capture what instinct couldn't.

Shaken by the encounter, it crouched low, not knowing its next move. Finally, after a long moment, it slinked off the roof, leaving confidence in its wake, sitting in stunned silence as the wind whistled through the landscape, singing its ghostly song. After scenting the air again and cautiously prowling to the front of the cabin, it sat at the doorway before moving inside.

Alice, hearing the commotion on the roof, wondered what was happening, she couldn't understand why the cougar was on the roof? What drove him there? She heard the big cat screaming, wailing and then shrieking. Concentrating, her ears grew attuned to the sounds, and if she didn't know any better, confusion and outright terror were now the cat's companion. *But what was causing it?* The cat was in agony, and yet there wasn't any other sound coming from the roof. She was so focused, she forgot about the towel rod in her hands. *Should she risk going to the front door and locking it?* Besides, there may be another animal out there waiting for her. She had to get a hold of herself, quit thinking of horrors confronting her, visions manifesting with supernatural creatures. There wasn't any such thing, but then again, why was the mountain lion acting this way. It was quiet again. If she was going to make her break, it was now. Holding the towel bar in her right hand for protection, she quietly unlocked the door. Pushing it ajar, her vision filled with the cougar bounding through the front door. *Oh God!* She thought. Quickly closing and locking the door again she waited for the inevitable.

The cat, seeing its prey, attacked the bathroom door again, growling in its rage. Still shaken and disoriented by the hostile encounter outside, it was troubled. Clawing at the door, it sensed something in the distance growing close. Out of his peripheral vision, he could feel the same sky blue eyes haunting him from across the room. The growl of the creature grew deeper and more threatening. Sensing danger with ears flattened, the mountain devil turned and sprang, slamming against the fireplace. Burning its hind paws from the hot coals, it cried out in surprise and pain before it bounded across the floor to the snow outside. Dragging hot coals in its wake, the big cat sat in the snow, bewildered, licking his paws and peering back at the cabin. Spooked from the vision, the silver devil wandered into the night. The last thing it saw, was a pair of sky blue eyes peering at him from behind a line of orange, growing on the floor.

TWENTY-THREE

Reunion

After the hunters trekked down the mountainside they helped Humberto finish dressing out the rams. It was hard work and little was said until the job was completed. Afterward they buried the carcasses deep in the snow and hung orange identification markers for the consignment crew to find the packages. They weren't interested in this part of the operation; there goal was to get the racks to the taxidermist as soon as possible. After preparing the trophy heads for travel, the group cleaned their cutting equipment in the snow and packed the rest of their gear before grooming the site. They wanted to make sure to leave the area the way they found it, clean and pristine, but with the scent of humans. The hunters were particularly careful in their efforts to keep other predators away.

"What time is the helo arriving tomorrow?" Leroy asked.

Jim looked at his son before answering, still cleaning his blade in the snow. "About eight in the morning. But we need to get going now. It's already getting toward dusk, and we still have a couple of miles to the rendezvous point."

Leroy nodded, "good idea."

With powerful LED head lanterns guiding their way the hunters moved south. The weather had turned colder, and snow started to fall in earnest as the hunters made their way through the high valley. Their destination was Davidson Point, at an elevation of ten thousand feet. The area afforded a good landing and takeoff site. The snow wasn't as deep, with stands of spruce and aspens, partially sheltering the wind from drifts; it was perfect for an overnight stay. As the hunters moved to the rendezvous point a scream echoed through the valley.

"What's that?" Clyde asked.

"Probably a mountain lion complaining about his meal," Earl said.

"Yeah, he either missed his dinner or it doesn't suit his liking. Damn cats, always disturbing the peace and never happy about their catch." Jim turned to Earl and was about to speak again when another cry sliced through the silence like a knife. This one seemed much closer but still directionless. "Anyone have an idea where it's coming from?" Jim asked, looking around.

"Too many objects for it to bounce off." Humberto surmised. "We need to get closer."

"Well, you might want to get closer, but I just want to get to the rendezvous." Jim said, trying to pinpoint the sound's direction.

Then, in the still of the night, it happened. A sound like no other rolled across the valley, shattering like glass in the darkness. High pitched and piercing in tone, a cry filled the night air with terror riding its currents. The men, stunned, turned and peered into the void.

"What the hell was that?" Earl asked. "If I didn't know any better, it sounded like an anguished cry of a woman or child."

Humberto rubbed his heavy black stubble and thought for a moment. "It sure was. I think someone is in trouble, and we need to investigate."

Another cry, lower, almost a growl, came rumbling across the valley floor toward the hunters. The men unslung their rifles and faced each other.

"Bert, how far away is it?" Jim asked.

"About a mile. I think it's coming directly at us from the west side of the valley, and it appears to be at the same elevation we're at."

Jim dropped his backpack, reached into one of the pockets and collected his portable GPS and lined up the coordinates while Earl pointed a flashlight for better illumination. Going from satellite to ground view, he could see a dot on the brightly lit screen that indicated some sort of structure. He switched screens for more information, and could see they were just a mile shy of the object.

"It looks like a house or cabin, and it has an address off High Valley Lane." Jim turned to Humberto. "Bert, isn't there a steep embankment leading from the west side of the valley a little less than a mile away?" He could see concern reflecting across his friend's face.

"Sure is. Let's drop our gear, mark the location, and take what we need. Time isn't on their side, and whoever it is needs our help. Jim, I have a bad feeling about this."

"I do too."

The men went about collecting what they needed.

Afterward, Clyde planted an orange pole marker in the snow and they quickly moved toward the embankment. Along the way, the hunters heard more screams as they approached the steep hill.

They fanned out for safety, not knowing what to expect. Once at the embankment, Jim and Earl climbed the rocky outcropping while Humberto, Leroy, and Clyde covered them from below.

After the first two reached the top, the other three climbed up. All five could now smell smoke in the air. The last few minutes had brought silence and uneasiness as the men determined what to do next. Jim and Earl would explore the structure while the other three covered them.

As Jim and Earl drew closer, they could see the cabin on fire through the trees. Heavy smoke roiled, hurricane-like, out through the front door. Jim yelled out. "Is anyone there?" Nothing, he yelled again.

A voice filled with terror cried out, "help me."

Jim and Earl ripped off their heavy coats, and Jim used them as a shield going through the door. He yelled again, "Where are you?"

With tears streaming down her face, Alice answered, "I'm in the bathroom. Is the cougar gone?"

"Ma'am, he's long gone." Jim went to his knees to get more oxygen. "We need to leave now! Come out and crawl to my voice."

The air was warm and sticky with smoke, and it was getting difficult for Alice to breath. *Was the voice real?* She was terrified and didn't know if the cougar was really gone. She thought of Frank out in the wilderness alone. Her life was flashing in front of her and she had to make a decision. Leave and take her chances, or stay and die. Alice jerked the ax from the door, crawled out of the bathroom and worked her way toward the voice. She reached out and found another hand in the thick, sooty smoke. Jim grabbed her arm and pulled her toward him, just as the two back windows exploded from the heat. In tow, he led her to the porch with Earl's help, and they tumbled in the snow before running to safety.

TWENTY-FOUR

Crevasse

Frank awoke, bruised and battered. It was pitch black and he felt disoriented, shivering in the dark. His arm felt better, though it was still sore. *What happened?* He asked himself. He was sliding down a steep slope, and now this. *Why is it so black?* He thought. Reaching into his coat pocket for his flashlight, excruciating pain nauseated him, radiating from his right side. *Oh God!* He must have broken some ribs. With panic setting in, he started to hyperventilate. The pain was now coming in waves. He had to get a hold of himself, or it would be the end of him. *Settle down and breathe slowly and evenly,* he told himself. After a few minutes, he felt better, and his thinking became clearer. He fought through the pain, and collected his inhaler, and took a few breaths. He was afraid to breathe too deeply because of his ribs, and he sure didn't need to have a coughing fit. After finding his flashlight, he snapped it on and looked around. His brown eyes blinked as he remembered. *My God! He had fallen into a crevasse.* Staving off panic he thought about what other injuries he had received. After checking, he found that he hadn't sustained anything serious.

Outside of his ribs, and his right arm he, was okay. *Cold comfort that was.* He was worried that he would not be able to make it to the top. Still lying on his back, he maneuvered to a different position and very slowly shrugged out of the rope holding his canvas bag. Even though it had been uncomfortable laying on it, he was glad that he had it. Undoubtedly, it had softened the impact. Shining the light around, he found he was on a ledge about ten feet wide, and the white jagged walls of the crevasse reached well beyond the beam to the opposite side. Looking up, he wasn't sure where the opening was, because the light ended, still reflecting the white walls of ice and snow. He knew the range of his flashlight was at least one hundred feet, and the opening was beyond that range. *What was he to do?*

Frank took stock of what he had. His snowshoes were still fashioned to his feet, and after further investigation, he had everything else except his walking stick. He must have let go of it right before going over the edge, or it fell over the ledge. His lance was lying nearby. *Thank God.* The tool could possibly help him get to the top. The metal tent stake was sharp and could be used for digging toes and handholds on the side of the walls. Scanning his environment again, he saw that the ice veered away from him, and as far as he could tell, there was no inward inclination. *Makes his climb much easier,* he thought. *Now, if he can fight through the pain to climb, he may have a fighting chance.*

Left with his own thoughts, he began to plan. Struggling through pain taking off his snowshoes, he wondered about the rope used as webbing for the shoes. Between both of them there must be at least thirty feet. *It would come in handy. But what would he do for the rest of the trip?* Once on top, he would have to rethread the snowshoes. Searching his backpack, he found his hunting knife, more rope, visquene, and his chemical hand warmers, among other things. His watch was broken, but he didn't care. He wondered if daylight reached this far down because it would be easier for his climb. He slid to the wall on the ledge and rolled the visquene out on the floor for some insulation, and changed his chemical hand warmers for his hands. His feet were another matter. He didn't know if he had enough strength to fight through the pain. He propped himself against the back wall and brought his legs up to reach his feet. For a big man, he was surprisingly limber, and after a time, he was able to change the chemical packs for his feet. Next, he cut some of the visquene into strips in order to bind his ribs and redo a sling for his right arm. The real test for pain was about to begin. Afterward, he mopped his heavy brow with the sleeve of his coat and broke down the webbing on his snowshoes. He needed to rest now in order to conserve his strength. He would worry about the other tasks later.

Staring into the pitch black, he thought about Alice and wondered if he would ever see her again. He hoped that she was okay and knew she relied on him to get to Telluride. *He had to make it.* Drifting off, a wolf appeared in his dreams again. Peering at him with sky blue eyes, he knew the creature wasn't threatening. Somehow, he got the feeling that the carnivore was looking out for his well-being. Frank didn't know why, but he felt he would see the night run again.

TWENTY-FIVE

The Fire

After Jim, Earl, and Alice reached the others, they turned and watched the cabin burn. The night sky lit up with a smoky, orange halo as flames shot into the void. Without a word, Jim wrapped his coat around Alice. He knew she was cold, only dressed in boots, jeans, and a long sleeve flannel shirt. Alice began to cry watching the family's vacation home go up in flames. *What else can go wrong,* she thought. The hunters gathered around her as Jim consoled her and gently questioned her about her situation.

"Oh my God! My husband," Alice cried. With tears streaming down her face, she told the hunters about Frank and their circumstances. After hearing this, Jim got on his sat phone and called 112 to contact local law enforcement authorities about Alice and Frank. After the call, Jim sat Alice down on a large spruce log nearby and questioned her further. He knew that anything would help. Even though Alice had told them that Frank would be traveling the road to Telluride, he didn't take any chances. He told Alice that an avalanche had occurred and that local authorities were investigating it.

"Where's the avalanche at?"

"It's somewhere near Mountain Way Road and the authorities are on their way to determine if the road is cut off."

"Oh, my God. My husband is traveling that road." Alice looked at Jim, "Oh Jesus! I hope he wasn't caught up in it."

Jim didn't want to upset Alice any more than she was, and said, "there's probably a good chance the avalanche had already occurred, and your husband happened upon it." He started to speak again, then answered his own question. "That means that there is a good possibility that Frank headed due south across country if the snow slide couldn't be traversed." In his concern, he almost forgot to tell everyone that a helo was being sent.

Silence descended as everyone watched the cabin burn to its cinder block foundation. Earl turned to Alice and asked if they had any shovels. Alice told him that the snow shovel was on the front porch, but she thought there were a couple of spades in the shed out back. Earl, Clyde, and Leroy headed around back to the shed, giving the cabin a wide berth. They hoped it wasn't burning along with the house. They were in luck. The work shed was far enough away and was spared from the fire. Leroy picked up a rock and bashed the lock on the door until it gave way. Earl and Clyde went inside, and sure enough, there was a spade and a flat blade shovel, and other tools they could use.

On their way out of the shed, Clyde spotted some tracks leading to the cabin. Following them to the edge of the hot coals and ash, he guessed they were wolf tracks by their size and pattern. He squatted on his snowshoes to get a better look.

Shallow in the snow, they were very large, and he surmised that he was looking at an extremely large wolf, about one hundred and forty pounds or so. *But why were the tracks so shallow?* He asked himself. The consistency of the snow and the depth of the paw prints didn't add up. *How odd,* he thought. He looked up at Earl, standing next to him. "Do you see anything strange about these wolf tracks?"

"I don't know," Earl said as he peered down at the ground. "They do look a little irregular."

"No, they're not irregular–they're just plain weird." "What do you mean?" Earl asked.

Clyde stood to face his friend. "The size of the prints doesn't match the depth. We're looking at a very large wolf here, but the tracks are too shallow to indicate this."

"I suppose so," Earl said.

As the two continued shoveling snow onto the hot ash and coals, they were careful, looking for more tracks. Leroy motioned them to another spot at the back of the cabin. "What are these?"

Clyde peered at them closely, and after a long pause, looked at Earl and Leroy. "If I didn't know any better, I'd say these are mountain lion tracks. Here, look at the heel pads. See the three lobes below. That's a cougar, and he's a big one." Clyde was pretty sure it was a male because of the size and depth of the prints, plus there wasn't any smaller tracks around to indicate cubs.

Earl turned to Clyde with a quizzical look in his brown eyes. "What's going on here? The cougar tracks are much deeper in the snow, and yet they are approximately the same size of the wolf prints, and both appear to be made at the same time."

"I'm not sure, but I think we have some questions that need to be answered." Clyde, looking at clear imprints of both sets of tracks in front of him continued. "There's a lot happening here or rather, the lack of that doesn't add up. Indeed, both sets look to be fresh and in close proximity to each other, and yet I haven't seen any scuffle marks, fur, or blood. Something strange is going on here, buddy."

Deep in thought, Earl rubbed the brown stubble on his narrow face. "I think we need to check with Jim and Humberto before we go any further. This is getting more bizarre by the minute." He pulled out his smart phone and took pictures of the scene.

"Maybe the woman can shed some light on this." Leroy added.

"Good idea," Earl said.

The three hunters walked carefully around the cabin, spotting more mountain lion tracks as they went. Even though some were partially obscured by the coals and ash, the men could see that they belonged to the same feline. The prints wandered in and out of the fire zone around the cabin, and eventually led to the smoky ruins of the front porch.

Jim padded Alice on the shoulder to console her before standing to face the three men approaching him. He could tell by their demeanor that their minds were troubled by something.

"What's going on?" Jim said as Humberto continued to sit with Alice.

"We're not sure, buddy." Clyde said as he motioned for Jim to step closer and out of earshot from Alice.

Jim looked at Clyde with a puzzled look on his face. "Now what is it?"

The other two hunters moved up to Clyde. "Did Alice tell you about a cougar and a wolf?" Clyde asked.

"Well, yes, about the cougar. After you guys left for the shed she told Humberto and I on how a cougar attacked her, but she didn't mention anything about a wolf. We're still not sure about why and how the cabin caught fire since she told us that she was locked in the bathroom the whole time. Now what's this about a wolf?"

"There's something strange going on, Jim." Clyde told him about what they had found. After discussing the situation at length, they decided to have Humberto accompany Clyde and Earl to the back for a closer look while Jim and his son, Leroy, question Alice further. After the three men headed toward the back of the burned-out cabin, Jim sat beside Alice again and waited.

"Has something happened at the back of the cabin? Is Frank back there?" She asked with a catch in her voice.

"No...no," Jim replied. "Nothing like that." Jim took a moment and looked at her again. He could tell that she was visibly upset–who wouldn't be. "Ah...ah the guys have spotted cougar tracks, and also another set of tracks that apparently belong to a wolf."

Alice looked at him in surprise. "A wolf?"

"Yep. Now, did you hear or see a wolf around the cabin?"

Leroy, standing nearby, interrupted. "Yeah, a wolf howling or growling."

With irritation flashing across his face, Jim held up a hand to quiet his son. Raking her fingers through her bleached blond hair, she puzzled at the question, thinking about any other sound besides the cougar. "No, didn't hear anything except the cat's scream."

"Are you sure?"

"Why do you ask? I think I would know the difference between a cougar's caterwaul and a wolf's howl. Besides, Frank and I heard screams the night before he left, and he said they were coming from a big cat–the same I heard earlier. Is there something I should be aware of? Wait a minute; we did see a wolf on the way to the cabin three weeks ago. It was standing on the road in front of the car, just staring at us. It was a huge gray creature with sky blue eyes. Frank said it was probably a wolf, but he had never seen one with blue eyes."

"Is there anything else?"

"Yeah, I got the strangest feeling from the animal, as if it wanted something–trying to tell me what it was. It was darn right chilling, and I could tell it in Frank's face too. Then it vanished in front of us."

"What do you mean–vanished?"

"It disappeared. One minute it was there, the next gone. Thinking about it now, it was as if the creature was using the driving snow as a camouflage."

"Why would it do that, and how come you refer to the wolf as creature?" Jim asked.

"Because it was almost supernatural in appearance." "What do you mean?"

"It's eyes and fur were different than any wolf I ever saw?"

Jim looked at his son again and discreetly motioned to cut it with the eyes. "Well, mam, I just wanted to verify what the guys had found. Nothing important. The main thing is that you're okay." Jim decided not to tell Alice about the conundrum with the wolf tracks– it could be checked later. Besides Earl and Clyde took pictures of the scene. "Anything else catch your attention?"

"Now that you mentioned it, there were a couple of things that struck me odd while I was in the bathroom." Alice hunched over and leaned on her elbows, thinking, before she answered. "I can't be sure, but I could've sworn I heard something up on the roof. I thought it was strange that the cougar would get up there. For what?"

"Perhaps he picked up another scent, maybe the wolf." "But why go up on the roof?" Alice asked.

"I don't know. Maybe the scent was up there."

"Another thing. After the cat reentered the cabin and dug its claws into the door again, it suddenly stopped, and the next thing I heard was a crashing noise and a scream. It sounded like it was coming from the back wall over by the fireplace."

"Interesting. Anything thing else?"

"No, that's it. The next thing I knew, I was hearing the sound of your voice."

Jim looked at her disheveled, bleached blonde hair and tear-streaked face, and could tell that she had gone through a lot in the last couple of weeks. Her blue eyes seemed tired, reflecting deep concern. He was also worried about Frank. Lord knows where he was by now. "Will find your husband," Jim said. "In fact, unless he fell in to a deep tree well, or some other happenstance we should be able to quickly locate him." As soon as he said this he bit his tongue. He should have known not to add any more wrought to the situation.

Alice looked at him with alarm written across her face. "I didn't think of any hazards out there except the deep snow and animals. God, I hope he's alright?" she blurted.

"He's fine, I'm sure of it. What you have told me about him it sounds like he can take care of himself." Jim looked at her again and measured her. "He's probably on the main road heading to Telluride by now."

Alice wasn't so sure. Dark clouds were now on the horizon of her mind, and distant shores were filled with horror in her thoughts. "Jim, thanks for the reassurance, but I'm not so sure.

He's like me, overweight and out of shape. Although, he has lost weight in the last couple three weeks and has toughened up. I just hope his skills carry him through."

Jim looked at her again and could tell she was deep in thought. He motioned Leroy to join the others. After his son left Jim walked toward the front of the cabin, searching for clues–anything would help. Besides, he needed to give the poor lady some space, time to think through all the events. He was still troubled by what Clyde had showed him. It just didn't make any sense. And what Alice said about the wolf she and her husband saw also didn't add up. By know the coals were cooling, and the only thing left to do was to complete the cleanup on any hot spots and wait for the mountain rescue crew to show up. The fire wasn't going anywhere, except out. As Jim was turning to walk back to Alice, he caught movement in his peripheral vision in the trees about seventy-five yards out. *A flash of gray,* he thought. *What was it? He wasn't sure, but it was quick and it was large.* Lumbering toward Alice and his rifle with his snowshoes, he yelled at her and the others.

TWENTY-SIX

Call Center

After receiving the 112 call, Denise Roberts consulted with her supervisor on how best to direct the request. She was concerned about the nature of the call. They usually received 911 calls and rarely had incoming satellite calls. The transmission was garbled and had a strange echo to it. She could clearly make out the name Alice, but the other name wasn't quite discernible, and it sounded like Francis, Franco, or possibly Frank. There was also something about hunters, but she couldn't determine what it was. The strangest thing about the incoming transmission was there wasn't any identification information attached to the call header such as the origination and number, and the name of the caller.

After further conversation with her supervisor, it was decided that they would call the mountain rescue unit to see who was registered for any type of activity on the mountain. Also, the call center would have the county check the property records for property owners in the San Juan Mountain range in and around Telluride. Denise was sure it was an urgent call and insisted that proper protocol was followed. After some checking it was determined that a Frank and Alice Thompson owned property on High Valley Lane, and upon further investigation they found that the Thompsons had flown into Telluride on December 18th.

There were also five hunters on the mountain permitted and registered to hunt Bighorn sheep. After having no luck in trying to reach the Thompsons and the hunters, it was finally decided to inform law enforcement officials in Telluride, San Miguel County Sheriff office and the mountain rescue team to gear up for a possible rescue operation. *Here it was a few days in to the New Year and things were already heating up on the mountain*, she thought. After putting down her Starbucks for the umpteenth time, she made the calls. She knew it would put in motion the equipment and personnel needed for the emergency. Since they found that there had been no communication between the Thompsons and their family during their Christmas vacation, the possibility existed that the Thompsons were marooned in their mountain cabin. Because of the urgency and the avalanche, a helo would be dispatched from the airfield to check on Frank and Alice Thompson and the hunters. And there was always the possibility that one or both of the Thompsons were trying to make their way back to Telluride.

And to add even more urgency to the mix, the National Weather Service just added an advisory that a Derecho may form over the San Juan Mountains in the next few hours. She didn't know what a Derecho was until she read the weather bulletin. It said it could get nasty with straight-line winds vectoring from the northwest to the southeast that could exceed one hundred miles per hour. With tall thunder heads marching on the storm front the area could experience a rare snow lightning event. Denise knew that they couldn't take any chances and had to cover all of their bases.

Earlier that morning a ground team had been sent to check on the exact location and size of the avalanche and now the Thompsons and hunters had been added to the list. A second team would be dispatched shortly because of the circumstances. To further add to the situation, she knew that a seismic alert had been issued yesterday for the Telluride, Colorado region, and that a team of scientists and engineers where on their way from the University of Colorado in Boulder. She wasn't sure, but she didn't think earthquakes were common in Colorado. On the other hand, her sister who lived in the Los Angeles area was an expert on them.

She hadn't felt anything yesterday, but local television coverage last night indicated that a quake had occurred yesterday at 0630 hours with the epic center 97 miles due south of Telluride, registering 4.9 on the Richter scale. *Not large by her sister's standard,* she thought, *but it was enough to get her attention.* Denise hadn't experienced this much tension around the call center since the forest fire three years ago.

TWENTY-SEVEN

Rescue Team

Art Sanders, a sergeant with the San Miguel County sheriff office had just received the additional information from his office via the car's radio a few second's ago. He turned to Doc Rivers a local geologists and Olaf Petterson, head of the mountain rescue unit. "Well boys it looks like our focus has changed somewhat. We are now searching for Frank and Alice Thompson and five hunters." Art went on and described the circumstances to his friends.

Doc sitting next to Art in the front seat of the county's SUV stowed the satellite photos of the avalanche he was looking at and shook his head. "You mean they're isolated and alone in their cabin?"

"Could be. But also they could be making their way back to Telluride and we have to be on the lookout for any telltale signs."

"What about the hunters? Olaf asked. "Nothing as yet, but we need to be mindful." "How well I know." Olaf said.

"Like I said a Guard helo has been dispatched and we should know within the hour." Art turned to Oly as he was making the turn off SR 50 onto Mountain Way Road. "I know if I was in their boots, especially with a Derecho coming I'd be freaking out."

"But how would they know." Doc chimed in.

"They wouldn't. And I bet if they're still there they are running low on food and fuel." Art ventured.

Doc ran a hand through his dark hair and thought for a moment. "There's more going on here–I just know it."

"Ya think!" Art exclaimed. "Look, there are no tracks coming off Mountain Way to the county road. It's been snowing, but not enough to entirely cover tire tracks in the last twenty-four hours."

Doc peered out the window to check Art's observation and said, "Looks like the snow field cut across the road somewhere up ahead. From the pictures, I'd say about five miles.

All three fell into silence thinking about what they might find as Art drove on. Even though they were interested in acquiring information about the slide, their main objective now was to locate the Thompsons and the hunters. The most recent call from the sheriff's office indicated that Frank and his wife, Alice, had been stranded in their cabin for over two weeks off High Valley Lane and that there was a possibility the Thompsons might try and hike out–not a good assumption in Art's mind. *So far, there weren't any signs to be found on this day*, he thought.

"Doc what do think caused this? The news said an earthquake struck south of us yesterday morning. I don't believe I have ever heard of this since working for the county."

Doc looked out at the snowy landscape and tilted his hat back. "It's pretty rare, Art, but it can happen. Right now I'm interested in seeing this puppy. From the photos it looks absolutely huge and a 4.9 doesn't do it justice. Perhaps after seeing it we can gather some clues on how it was caused."

Olaf Petterson unwound his frame in the rear seat, leaned forward and joined the conversation. The big Swede was interested in how such a large snow slide could be created from a relatively small earthquake. He was the lead for the mountain rescue unit and gauging by Art and Doc's conversation, the size of the avalanche they were talking about was way outside of anything he had seen before. "Come on fellas, you're making a mountain out of a molehill. I've seen the pictures to ya know and it can't be that large."

"I don't know," Art said. "The area from the satellite photos sure got my attention, though the edges are hard to tell where the slide ends and the terrain begins."

"That's exactly my point. How do we know for sure," Olaf said. "I mean the borders look pretty fuzzy and nondistinct. It could be up to a mile long, and as far as the width and height who knows."

Doc interrupted their discussion. "Looks like we're about to find out."

As the county vehicle approached the snow slide, all three stared at the huge white mound with amazement. Art was careful to park the car a good two hundred feet away, being mindful of not disturbing any tracks that may be nearby. Their mission was not only to gather information about the snowfield, but also to find the Thompsons and hunters. Three other mountain rescue team members and a city deputy had already been dispatched for backup.

"Indeed it is a mountain," Doc said as he exited the vehicle.

Oly peered in both directions and could see that it gradually disappeared into a curtain of snow and ice. After exiting the Ford Escape's rear door, he turned to Art and said, "It goes on forever and it's at least 100 feet high and who knows how wide it is."

"Yeah, and look at the boulders and trees everywhere. It's a mess," Doc added.

Art looked at them and nodded. "Okay fellas, first things first. Snows pickin' up and we need to see if we can locate any footprints before the snow erases any traces. I want to know if the Thompsons and the hunters are on this side of the avalanche.

While we are waiting for backup, Doc, I want you to search the downside of the slope and report back in forty-five minutes." Art turned to Petterson. "Oly, you do the same on the upslope. In the meantime, I'll check for prints around here." As he watched his two friends head back to the car to collect their snowshoes Art knew that it was unlikely they would find any tracks coming off the snow slide and heading east on the road. The snowfield looked almost impassable because of the size of the debris field. If they were going to find tracks, it would mean the prints were made before the avalanche occurred. He knew the other team would be arriving soon and their task would be to try and traverse the snow slide and look for footprints in the snowfield and on the other side. *Now if only the snow would let up to give them a decent chance,* Art thought.

While his friends were checking the snow slide, Art scanned the road and snow bank for any tracks. After searching the area for a while he was no further along than he was when he first arrived, except the snowfall had increased. Just then Doc came trudging back after searching the south side of the avalanche. Ice crystals clung from his neatly trimmed dark beard as white clouds of air exhaled from his mouth. He sat on the nearest rock to gain respite before speaking.

"Did you find any footprints?" Art asked

"No, just a set of mountain lion tracks about half a mile down pointing toward the snow field. They looked to be going in a zigzag manner up slope and they were huge. I'm guessing we are looking at a male cat that's well over two hundred pounds."

"That's all we need." Art said. "Doc, are you packing?" "No, I thought I'd leave the heavy lifting to you." "You're qualified, right?"

"Yeah, who isn't around here?"

"Go get the spare Glock in the glove box. The clip is in and the safety is on." While Doc was retrieving the gun, Art looked around once more to see if anything was amiss. *Wouldn't want any uninvited guests sneaking up.* He shouted at Doc, "Were you able to locate the end of the slide?"

"No, and I have to tell you this is one large mass of snow, trees and rock. And from the information we have received on the Thompsons, I don't believe, if they were on this road, they could have made it across. Never seen anything like it."

Art took off his snow goggles to clean them and wiped his forehead. "The section around the road and slide area on this side is clean of footprints except for our own. You're right if the Thompsons were heading this way, the avalanche would have stopped them and they would have had to head south along the other side. Once they cleared the snowfield, they could head due east to the county road. That goes for the hunters too. I know that's what I would do if I made it this far."

Art and Doc peered north along the snow slide and could see a large figure emerging through a white wall of snow and ice. Snow had intensified since the three had left the warm confines of the county vehicle and was trying its best to bury any fresh tracks in the snow.

"Any luck?" Doc yelled out.

"No, nothing. Couldn't even find the end of the snowfield–must go on forever." Olaf lumbered up to the two smaller men standing next to a large boulder. "Went up about a half a mile, looking for footprints and finally turned back. The height of the field appeared to be diminishing at that point, but still couldn't see the end of it–snows coming too hard. Any luck on your end?

"Spotted some large cougar tracks–that's all," Doc said. "Are you armed?" Art asked.

"Of course," Olaf replied.

Art retrieved the radio from his coat pocket and called his office. He wanted to know when the second team would be arriving–they should have been here by now. He was worried about the deteriorating conditions burying any evidence of the Thompsons or the hunters. He knew the weather had been extremely cold and snowy for the last three weeks and had only momentarily let up in the last couple of days, but looking up he could see that it was about to change–they had to hurry.

TWENTY-EIGHT

The Climb

Visions rushed to his mind, mixed with gray and blue. Was he experiencing the sky, breaking with cumulus and shafts of light?

Gray, Frank thought as his consciousness snapped open. He stirred from his slumber and peered straight up and caught the sight of beautiful gray. Overjoyed by the feeling of euphoria, Frank now knew that he wasn't in total darkness and probably not too far from the surface. *But what was the blue?* He thought. Was it water instead of land? How could that be? Everyone likes the blue. He knew that. Gray was good too. Either way, it meant getting out of this God-forsaken hell hole. Blue remained at the back of his mind as he sat up and shook sleep from his eyes. He didn't need any help; ribs shooting in pain chasing sleep away he came full circle as he grunted in discomfort.

Frank carefully reached and grabbed his lance to help prop himself on the crevasse's back wall. He shifted around to collect the visqueen, folded it and placed it out of the way. He didn't want a slick surface to work on. After finishing the last half sandwich, he changed the chemical heat packs for his feet and hands. He decided that he didn't need his makeshift snowshoes anymore. *Too much weight to carry,* he thought, and tossed them aside. Next, he discarded the canvas bag. The food was gone and there wasn't much anything else of value. He needed to climb light. Tying the ends of the rope together from the snowshoes he thought on how to make the climb to the top and why he needed the rope. Somehow he knew that it would come in handy and he wasn't going to leave without it. Easy wasn't in his vocabulary, but with his lance and hunting knife it gave him a fighting chance.

The eyes kept haunting him from the edges of his mind.

Now he remembered, they were blue, the bluest blue he had ever seen. But what or who was behind those eyes–he couldn't quite remember. He only knew that he had seen them before, especially when he was a child and on the road to the cabin. He had the feeling he wasn't alone and somehow this thing would be helping him. The snow crumbled in icy flakes as he worked his lance, digging foot and handholds into the white, nearly vertical wall. He guessed he had over seventy feet to the top, and he was glad for some light. He hoped his right arm would hold as he slowly made his way up the crevasse. He felt icy flakes and snow drifting from above. Looking up again, he could now see an outline of a shaggy figure peering down at him with radiating sky blue eyes. It was perfectly still, emerging out of the gray or was he the gray? Frank couldn't tell.

Scenting the air, the wolf looked around feeling alone except for his friend below. He didn't know what had happened or if he could help. Did wolves help? He wasn't sure, but he knew he had to do something. The creature paced back and forth as if looking for something. Was he trying to find himself, trying to see who he was or what he was? Again the splitting haunted him. He sniffed the gouge marks in the snow. It was faint, but he recognized it as the same scent he had encountered yesterday standing atop the snowfield. He looked down at his friend again. Continuing to search, he spotted a small scraggly-looking spruce next to the crevasse, its trunk partially uprooted from the never- ending mountain wind. With a running leap the creature hit the tree and with his momentum and weight, carried the small tree across the crevasse and landed with the tree on the other side. The carnivore rolled off the branches and skidded to a halt. He had felt motionless in flight and then it just happened. How was he able to do this? Was it instinct or imagination? He only knew that the tree now formed a bridge to survival for his friend.

Chunks of snow came crashing down on Frank causing him to nearly lose his footing. He held on thinking was there another avalanche? After a moment or two he ventured to look up and to his surprise he could see something lying across the opening. It looked like a small tree with branches askew and snow still crumbling down. *Who or what caused this? Why?* Frank thought as he struggled to re-secure his hold on the crevasse's wall. After catching his breath from the pain in his ribs and waiting for the last of the snow to fall he yelled out. "Help! Is anyone there?" He listened intently for a reply, any reply. He ignored the pain and yelled again. Silence like a glider's wake greeted him once more.

He was halfway up the crevasse and surly his voice would have carried to the top. He yelled one more time–nothing. Uncoiling the rope from around his waist, he looked up again and could see a pair of sky blue eyes and a gray outline of a wolf, still, against the background of a slate gray sky. Frank couldn't believe what he was seeing. It was strange and surreal–the same picture he was dreaming about the other night and long ago. *Could it be the same wolf,* he thought. For that matter it could be almost anything or nothing. His mind couldn't grasp the image he was seeing. It was there but wasn't there. It looked almost like an etch-a-sketch with a steel gray background. The creature was pulsating, changing direction as he peered at it. It was on one side of the crevasse, and then the other without ever crossing or so it seemed. He was looking at the carnivore's fur, opaque needles against the gray background, moving, constantly shifting. And those sky blue eyes, penetrating, mesmerizing, beseeching him to come to the top. A chill came over Frank, not one of cold but of fright thinking about reaching the opening. *Was it just out of reach like everything else in his life?* He thought. No matter how hard he had tried he could never really succeed at anything. Sure he had a great family and they were comfortable. But what about him? He had always been told as a young man to reach higher, go for the stars and make his parents and relatives proud. But no one had really stepped forward to help him. Sure some couldn't financially but others could. *Isn't that what family is about?* Frank thought. He had to go it alone, pay for what few college classes he took. And then there had been the expense of books and transportation. He found that he really didn't like school anyway. Perhaps he had been taking the wrong major for his abilities. He didn't know since he wasn't getting help–anywhere. No one stepped up–even for counseling or guidance.–it was a crock. Well, failure wasn't an option this time. Not for himself or for his family.

The wolf peered down at his friend, motioning for him to continue his climb. He was looking at the rope, willing his friend to toss it over the tree to help him reach the opening. He moved from side to side, whining for his friend's attention. One moment he was on one side of the crevasse, the next, the other. He didn't know if he could hear him or see him, but he had to try. Somehow he knew his friend was redemption. A key to unlocking how he came to be and who he was. The wolf peered down the crevasse again, staring at the figure below wondering if his friend sensed what he was trying to do.

Clearing his vision of the entity Frank shook his head and peered up at the ice walls trying to make sense of what he had just seen. The wolf, or rather the vision he had seen was gone. He had business to attend to. He untied the rope from his waist and held it out with his left hand, lowering it until he released enough length and heaved it toward the tree. It fell short. The chunk of ice he tied to the end of the rope had held. He figured he had to get at least ten feet closer to the opening before he would have any chance of looping the rope around the tree. The wall above him was inching inward and the climb would be difficult but he had to try. There was a small ledge twelve feet above his head and if he could make it he felt that he had a decent shot of circling the rope around the tree to help him leverage the rest of the way up. He used his knife to continue carving small holes into the wall.

Perilously, he clung to the ice, inching his way like a rock climber clings to a rock wall. He only wished that he had crampons and ice picks to aid his climbing. After another hour of extreme exertion, he reached his prize. The pain in his ribs was racking his body in waves of nausea by the time he maneuvered onto the small ledge. His right arm was throbbing as he slumped against the wall, chest heaving, straining for oxygen as his vision dimmed nearly to blackness fighting for reality. After it seemed like an eternity, Frank regained his vision and rested for a while to rebuild some of his strength. He looked up again and saw that the ice walls were angling in even more toward the top and his only hope was riding on his throwing ability. He was no stranger to fly- fishing and was excellent at casting and backcasting. But this was different; it was more of a heave than a cast. He stood sideways on the small ledge and untied the rope again from his waist and dangled it below him while gauging the length he needed to swing. It was a little too long so he looped another section around his waist. He extended his left arm parallel to the wall and moved it back and forth like a pendulum to gain momentum for the underhand toss. The crevasse narrowed perpendicular to him, but he had plenty of room to maneuver along the parallel axis and that's what he needed. The tree was slightly behind him and twenty feet above, and ran across the opening. His only hope was to heave the rope so it came over the top of the tree. He could then let out more line and let the weight of the ice chunk pull the twine to him. That was his plan–simple. He let go. The throw was perfect but the rope got caught in some of the branches and didn't make it over the top. He peered carefully at the tree and saw that there was a bare spot at the base of the spruce before the branches started. *What was he thinking; he should have known better,* he thought. He dug his feet into the ledge and tugged gently on the rope. Thank God he was able to release it. He braced for the impact as the twine and chunk of ice rocketed past. He knew the chunk only weighed about two pounds, but he wasn't taking any chances and girded for the tug. The next heave was spot on and he released the slack in the line and watched as the rope came toward him. After grabbing the end of the cord he untied the chunk of ice and surveyed the ice walls again above him. They angled in and were rough and jagged with a light layer of fresh snow lining the opposite wall the last ten feet to the surface. *When he got to that point, it would be like climbing a chimney.* Frank tested the rope. The tree dug into the snow and held. He swung out over the crevasse. He grunted as his chest and waist took the full weight of his body. His ribs were on fire and he almost panicked from the deep throbbing pain. Somehow he steadied himself by jabbing the lance into the nearest wall with his good hand and tried to relax–it was difficult. He had a plan. By gaining leverage with the lance he was able to climb the rope hand-over-hand until he reached a spot where the crevasse narrowed enough to where he could straddle the walls with his feet and continue to the top. Two hours later he was using the tree and the crevasse's opposite wall for leverage to boost him onto the snow. He was exhausted, sore and in pain but alive. For sometime, he lay motionless catching his breath and looking up at the slate gray sky. He figured it was late afternoon and the best afternoon of his life—he was alive! He still had his knife, lance and extra chemical heat packs in his coat pockets, and that was about it. Frank looked around for any signs of life—there wasn't any except for disappearing prints in the snow—the same tracks he recognized earlier.

TWENTY-NINE

The Encounter

Alice was startled as Jim streaked toward her, he yelled for her to get down next to the large log she was sitting on. The big cat was now only twenty yards out and closing fast. As Jim reached for his rifle he ducked below the log as the cougar leaped across with the gun barrel grazing the cougar's underside. Leroy hearing the commotion was the first to come around from the back of the cabin as the silver devil scrambled to its feet and started to make its turn toward Jim. Leroy screamed to deflect the cat's attention. It worked. The cougar turned and eyed its prey with its sandy-gold eyes, growling and hissing. Only then, Leroy realize he was armed with only a flat blade shovel. The cougar hunched its powerful hind legs and sprang. Leroy anticipating stepped to the side and grunted as he brought the full force of the shovel to the side of the cat's head. The cougar screamed as it skidded to the ground, blood pouring from its ear. It turned and eyed its adversary warily, sizing him up. By now Alice could see that Clyde and Humberto had reached the front of the cabin and took in the scene in front of them. It was crazy. Leroy and the mountain devil were circling one another, embraced in a deadly dance of death looking for an opening. Humberto had his Weatherby at ready waiting for an opportunity to take the big cat down as Jim approached from the other side. The cougar looked at the two hunters behind him and the one in front and screamed again. It felt trapped as it backed toward the burnt foundation of the cabin eying its prey. The air still heavy with smoke the cat continued to back away from the hunters. Partially obscured now, it turned and scampered over a small log and was gone. Humberto fired but was too slow to match the cat's reflexes and missed.

Besides the Weatherby wasn't set up to work at this range. Jim stood and watched as the animal bounded into the trees and disappeared behind thick foliage. As Alice approached him he turned and asked if she was okay.

"I'm fine, but I'm wondering if it's the same cat that was in the cabin earlier?"

"Can't say," Jim said. "Only thing I know for sure is he's a big boy."

Jim turned to his son and said, "Some nerve you've got. Don't you know you could've been killed–that was a big cat."

Leroy deflected the question. "Why didn't you shoot, dad?

You had 'em in your sights."

Jim peered out to where the cougar went into the brush. "I don't know. It just seemed weird seeing a gray flash jump back into the trees."

"What are you getting at?" Humberto asked.

Jim thought for a long moment. "I mean that cougar is somehow connected to those strange wolf prints and I want to know what he knows."

Clyde chuckled. "Just exactly how are you going to do that, ask him?"

"No, of course not," Jim said as he gave his friend an angry look. "We need to get that cat and look for any evidence of contact with the wolf. Outside of his damaged ear compliments of my son, I didn't see anything else on him–he looked clean."

Silence descended on the group as they all turned and stared up through the thinning veil of smoke, searching for the approaching helo. Jim yelled at everyone to collect whatever gear they had and follow him down the embankment to the valley below. That's where he was instructed to take the group. One by one they climbed down the hill covering each other and went to the orange marker. After the hunters collected the rest of their gear, they all headed toward a high spot in the valley where the chopper was supposed to land. The cougar was long gone and Alice wondered what was next.

THIRTY

The Search

A rt Sanders motioned to Doc Rivers the geologist as another car came up the road toward them. Olaf Petterson the lead rescue mountaineer muttered under his breath, "It's about time." By now the county sheriff was issuing orders on the radio as the big SUV parked next to their rig. Three mountain rescue team members came scrambling out and went to the rear of the vehicle for additional gear. After fetching their equipment, they walked over to where Art and his team were standing with snowshoes in hand and said their hellos before getting down to business.

Introductions weren't really necessary since they knew each other. Art was the first to speak. "Abe, what took you guys so long?"

Abraham Silvers was a burly, rough looking fellow and a person you didn't want to meet in a dark alley. He was one of the leads and a veteran with the mountain rescue team, and was always direct and to the point. "We had to turn back and collect some additional gear after finding this morphed into a search party for the Thompsons and the hunters. We initially set out to give you guys backup for inspecting the avalanche. I guess there was some miscommunication with the 911 dispatcher to begin with.

So what's going on?"

Art looked at the three arrivals in front of him and paused to collect his thoughts before starting. Besides Abe there was Steve Lawrence a relatively new member of the mountain rescue unit, and a shorter man standing next to Steve was Angel Garcia, the unit's communication guru. "Well, since we arrived we have searched at least a half a mile in both directions on this side of the snow slide and haven't found anything except a pair of large cougar tracks that Doc spotted on the south end of his search."

"Yeah, and the tracks were heading across the avalanche. I don't know what that cougar was thinking, but I'm sure he had a rough go of it." Doc said with a grin.

Art looked at the snow mass in both directions before he continued. "Okay, boys, the latest information we received is that the Thompsons are most likely stranded in their cabin and a helo will be dispatched to check on them and probably bring them back to Telluride. In the event that they are heading down the mountain we're here to find them. Also, we are supposed to check on the hunters if we find them. If the Thompsons did leave their cabin it's unlikely that they crossed the snowfield or headed north away from Telluride." Looking at Abe, Art continued. "Just to make sure I want you and Steve to cross the avalanche here and head north. Doc, I want you and Oly to head south on this side of the snowfield and Angel and I will cross over here and head south on the other side and we'll meet up where the slide ends. I have a hunch, if they're out here, we will find them somewhere south of here. Everyone has their radios, probe poles and are you armed?" They all nodded. "Be vigilant in case you encounter the cougar.

Also, the information I received didn't mention that the Thompsons had a rescue beacon so these probes may come in handy." Art checked his watch. "Is there anything else?" Everyone was silent. "Okay, snap on your shoes and get crackin'."

The snow had been increasing for the last couple of hours and the team knew they were racing against the oncoming storm and darkness. As Art and Angel began their trek across the snowfield, Art peered at the size of the boulders and trees scattered about. He couldn't believe what he was seeing. The news said the quake was a 4.9 on the Richter scale, but looking at the debris field the reading should have been higher. "Angel, what do you make of this?" Art asked.

"From what I'm seeing with uprooted trees and boulders and the size of this snowfield, in my estimation, it would take a much larger earthquake than what was reported."

"My thoughts exactly, Angel. What do you think is going on?" Art asked.

"I don't know, but I'm sure we'll find out."

As the two trekked on they fell into their own thoughts thinking about the Thompsons and the hunters. It took them an hour to traverse the snowfield and head south. Art radioed the other team members to check on their progress and to see if there was anything of interest. There wasn't. After traveling about a mile the snowfield finally ended and they could see Lake Timothy off in the distance. Art knew the terrain and knew it was a frozen expanse of five hundred acres of water.

"Angel, stop." Art pointed to his right. "If I didn't know any better I think we just found tire tread marks."

"Tire treads?" Angel said as he peered at the indentation in front of him. "How come tire marks are clear out here?"

Art looked at the treads again. "You know I saw some pock marks in the snow along the side of the snowfield a way back and wasn't sure what they were until now. I needed some confirmation and now I think I know."

"What's that?"

"I think we have a lone person hiking out here with makeshift snowshoes fashioned out of tires and those snow divots next to the tire marks indicate he is using some kind of lance or pole."

"Why didn't you say something before?"

"Wanted to make sure. It could've been almost anything, but now with what I'm seeing it makes sense. Let's move on and see if we can find more tread marks before the snow hides all evidence."

The two men trudged on through the deep snow on their snowshoes looking for more marks. They weren't sure what direction the tire treads were moving in and only hoped that more clues would be provided as they got closer to the lake. They had to hurry or otherwise the falling snow would obliterate any tracks that were left. As they got closer to the frozen expanse they saw more tread and pock marks in the snow but nothing that would indicate the direction the lone figure was traveling. After arriving at the lake they discovered more divots and tread marks at the edge of the lake. Angel squatted on his snowshoes and carefully studied a group of indentations in front of him. It appeared that some of the tread marks had a square backing to them and that someone was testing the thickness of the lake's surface. "Art come on over here, I think I've found something."

Art moved to where Angel was standing and could see gouge marks in front of him. "Do you think he crossed the lake?"

Angel looked through his field glasses at the white expanse, and even though snow was falling he could see at least a couple of hundred feet out and answered, "I don't think so. There's no sign of tire treads out there, and if he didn't have GPS he could get lost very easily." Angel turned to Art and continued. "If I'm not mistaken the main road to Telluride is due east of the lake and I think he's headed in that direction."

Art retrieved his GPS and dialed in Lake Timothy. "You're right, highway 50 is a mile and a half due east of here." Art looked up as Doc and Oly finally arrived from the north side of the avalanche. "What took you guys so long? We've been waiting here for twenty minutes," Art chided.

Doc looked at Oly and took the lead. "We were careful–didn't want to miss anything."

"Did you find any footprints or anything else?" Angel asked.

"No, just the cougar tracks I mentioned earlier." Doc replied.

"That's odd," Art added.

"What do you mean?" Oly asked.

"I mean if the cougar was crossing the snowfield, where is he? We didn't see any tracks on our side of the avalanche. Either the cat is still somewhere in the snowfield or the snowfall has obliterated his prints. However, we did find some tread marks from a tire."

Doc and Oly looked at each other with puzzled looks before Doc spoke. "What do you mean by tread marks?"

Art led Doc and Oly to the lake's edge where Angel had spotted tread marks and indentations in the ice. "What do you make of this?" He asked.

Oly squatted on his snowshoes for a closer look and examined them closely. "I see what you mean by tire marks and those divots over there on the ice were made with a sharp object–probably a knife or something similar. Do you see how the ice is chipped at an angle and the marks run relatively deep into the ice?" Before anyone could answer, Oly continued. "It looks like someone was testing the ice to see if it was safe to travel across." Oly stood and peered out across the lake, searching for tracks. He was a big man, well over six feet with a shock of blond hair and expressive blue eyes. His grandparents had emigrated from Sweden and eventually made their home in Denver. "Did you spot any tread marks on the way here?" Oly asked.

"Yeah, every few hundred feet or so." Art said. "And were they heading toward the lake?"

"We're not sure." Art pointed to the tire marks at the lake's edge.

"Oly, you see the square edges on this one?"

Oly turned to where Art was pointing. "Ya, I see what you mean. It appears that the person rocked back on his snowshoes when he or she was testing the ice." Oly looked at the tread marks again. "Art, this has to be Frank Thompson. I mean there's no way the hunters would be using makeshift snowshoes."

"Yeah, that's my thinking too." Art said.

While Olaf discussed the new findings with the others, Art radioed the Sheriff's Office and spoke with his superior, Captain Jason Whitfield about what they had found. They both agreed that Frank Thompson had probably left the cabin to seek help. The captain told the sergeant that a Guard Blackhawk helicopter would be arriving soon to the Thompson's cabin, but to continue the search for Frank Thompson. He also indicated that a small command center was being set up in the Sheriff's Office to coordinate efforts between them, the State Police, Telluride Police Department and the Mountain Rescue Unit. The captain was not only concerned about the Thompsons but also the five hunters.

He knew they were experienced outdoorsmen, especially with Jim Hazelton leading the party. The captain also knew about Jim's reputation of being a world-class hunting guide, but he was concerned about the approaching storm. If the storm turns into a Derecho as the National Weather Service feared all bets were off.

After Art broke the connection with the captain he radioed Abe and Steve to give them further instructions and to update them on what they had found. Afterward he turned to the rest of the group and said, "I think Frank Thompson is heading east toward the main county road."

"How do we know it's Frank?" Angel asked.

Art leveled his brown eyes at Angel while considering his last statement. "Who else would it be?" He paused again to reflect on what he was going to say next. "I'm sure whoever it is, he or she will need our help. Besides, it won't be long before we know for sure. The captain will radio me as soon as he gets word from the Guard crew."

The four men turned east and headed toward the highway.

Dusk was upon them and time was running out. Art received another transmission from the other team members heading north along the avalanche reporting that they had reached the end of the snowfield and still no footprints or tread marks, and no signs of Frank Thompson. Art told Abe and Steve to search the east side of the avalanche on their way back to the rigs, and then wait for further instructions. He again informed them of the approaching storm and told them not to dally. It would be another hour or so before they reached the county road and he was worried about Frank. It was getting dark and the storm was moving in. He hoped that they would find him in time.

Rescue

I t was dusk by the time the hunters were halfway to the high spot on the valley floor. Alice could hear the approaching sound change in pitch and intensity as they neared the landing area. The group could see searchlights descending through the gloom as the sound grew louder. Even though it was nearly dark, Humberto recognized the helo's sound from his military training. It was a Sikorsky Blackhawk and most likely sent by the Colorado National Guard. Billowy white clouds of snow, created by the wash of the rotors surged in all directions as it touched down. As the group approached, it powered down and Alice could see two National Guard members exiting the bird. They moved out of the wash and motioned toward the hunters. The group waved at the guard, as they got closer. Alice, Clyde, Earl and Leroy hung back and Alice watched as Jim and Humberto went to greet the two crew members.

Jim was still troubled by what he had heard from the other four hunters. He hadn't had time to look behind the cabin because of all the commotion with the cougar and the short window to meet the helo, but he was still curious to see what was back there. He and Humberto had already talked and decided to stay on the mountain and track down the cougar. Besides they hadn't brought along the Bighorn trophies since they had a helo coming in the morning, and this would also afford them time to look for Frank. With all the gear they had and with six additional people, the Blackhawk would've been crowded. Jim and Humberto had already made up their minds and traveling lightly would give them the opportunity of getting to the cougar quickly.

After a long discussion with the helo crew, it was decided that they could stay but to keep in contact with the San Miguel County Sheriff's office. After the two hunters said their goodbyes to the others and Jim retrieved his coat and helped Alice snap off her snowshoes, Jim and Humberto stood and watched from the perimeter of the backwash as the Blackhawk lifted off. After the helo left, Jim turned to Humberto and said, "Bert, let's head back to the cabin before the snow hides all the tracks. I need to see what is back there."

"Well, let's get moving then–the storm isn't going to wait for us." Humberto slung his rifle over his broad shoulders and then rubbed his black stubble before heading toward the cabin.

Jim followed his friend toward the embankment, He knew there wouldn't be much conversation with his friend because Humberto was the quiet sort, but very intense with his actions and his deeds. You could always count on Bert, whether it be in the mountains or anywhere else. The man was a rock.

After reaching the top of the rise, they proceeded slowly to the smoldering remains of where the cabin once stood. Cautious again because of fresh cougar tracks, they knew the big cat was hanging around. Under ordinary circumstances they wouldn't bother, but they wanted to get at the cat to see if there was any evidence of a wolf's encounter. For some reason Jim had to know. Was it because of his childhood dreams of a huge gray wolf and the little omega or was it something more ominous? He had a feeling that he was about to find out. The beams from their flashlights and headlamps cast contrasting energy sources of light across the snowy landscape–the halogen yellows from their flashlights fighting the LED blues from their headlamps for dominance. As the hunters spotted more cougar tracks in front of them their rifles were at the ready. Humberto, with his reliable Weatherby 300 Magnum and Jim with his trusted Winchester 270 weren't taking any chances. As they moved to the back of the cabin's cinder block foundation they could see that the tool shed was scorched but still standing. Thankfully a line of tall Colorado blue spruce sheltered the animal tracks in the snow. They could tell the storm was moving closer because the wind was intensifying and shifting, coming from the north. Jim knew they were running out of time and he quickly got down to business scanning the ground in front of him while Humberto kept a wary eye out for the cougar. Even though there was a thin layer of snow on top of the tracks, he could tell the cougar prints looked normal with size matching the depth of the cat's tracks. The wolf was a different story though. The print size was far larger than what the depth should have indicated. He was puzzled as the other hunters had been by this discovery.

"Bert you're right, these wolf tracks don't make sense." Jim stood and looked off into the distance past the shed. "Did anyone check to see where these tracks were coming from?"

"I believe Clyde went further back beyond the cabin to check. And, as far as I know there wasn't any difference."

"Did he find the end of the tracks?"

"What do you mean by that?" Humberto asked. "The tracks could have gone on forever until they disappeared into a creek, a canyon or something."

"That's true, but I would like to find out where it was crouching or resting."

Jim started to head past the shed looking. Humberto stood for a moment thinking before following his friend. "You know you may have a point. We may find some clues at his resting place."

As the two hunters followed the wolf's tracks, they disappeared and reappeared again in places where the ground was sheltered by trees. About a quarter mile past the shed they entered a very sheltered area surrounded with trees and could clearly see the tracks. But then a very strange thing happened–the hunters couldn't believe what they weren't seeing.

"Where are the tracks?" Jim asked. "They were here and now they're gone–vanished into thin air." Jim squatted again on his snowshoes and closely inspected the line of prints. As he peered in front of him, the depth of the tracks gradually diminished into nothing. "This can't be. I mean the falling snow could have blunted the tracks, but they were sharp, well defined and then they disappear? Are you seeing what I'm seeing?"

"Incredible!" Humberto exclaimed.

Jim fell silent as if in a trance, thinking about the little omega, and the huge gray wolf that had visited his dreams long ago. He remembered that he had named the little wolf Charlie because he was so cute and clumsy. He also often wondered, as a child, if the larger creature was really a wolf or something else.

Even though the outline had clearly been that of a wolf he could see through it. And those eyes, those sky blue eyes.

A high-pitched scream broke the silence. Jim used the butt of his Winchester for leverage and swung around on his snowshoes to face the sound. A picture of a huge gray cat bounding toward him out of the darkness filled his vision. He didn't have time to aim, only to plant the gun's stock firmly into the snow and wrap his thumb on the trigger. The silver devil leaped at its prey. Jim waited until the big cat came down on the barrel before he fired. The cougar slumped over him, twitching in the throes of death, its eye shine waning to a dull gray. Struggling to get out from under the big cat, Humberto waited until his friend was free and then ventilated the mountain devil with two 300-magnum rounds.

"My God!" Humberto exclaimed. "You were damn lucky, my friend. I've never seen you move so fast in your life."

"Yeah, it was pure instinct, Bert. I still don't believe it myself." Jim was sitting in the snow next to the cougar with his snowshoes pointing to the heavens looking every bit an amateur who had just fallen. He was so terrified that he was shaking.

"You okay, buddy?"

"Yeah, I'll be fine in a minute. Just need to calm down." "Man, you were like a Maasai warrior of old, killing a lion with a spear. That took guts."

"Bert, it wasn't guts just instinct–I just reacted."

"Some reaction, buddy."

Humberto sat next to Jim in the snow and looked at the big cat, shaking his head. He still couldn't believe what just happened. After a spell the two men got up and rolled the cougar over and extracted

Jim's gun. Outside of it being covered with the cougar's blood and gore, it looked intact. They both inspected the cougar and found that the kill shot was to the heart. The hunters then looked for signs on the body that would indicate a wolf attack but couldn't find any. Jim could see that the cat was unmarked except for the animal's damaged right ear compliments of his son and the kill shot. They cleaned Jim's Winchester as best they could, collected their Bighorn trophies at the bottom of the embankment and then set out to Davidson Point to meet the chopper in the morning. By now the snow was coming down in sheets driven by the north wind, and the temperature had fallen fifteen degrees in the last two hours. Visibility was near zero and the hunters had to constantly check their GPS to make sure they were on point. The going was slow and brutal and they were bone tired, and wanted to get to the rendezvous point. On the way they both fell into silence, one thinking about the encounter with the cougar, the other thinking about the huge gray wolf in his childhood dreams.

THIRTY-TWO

Guard Flight

"Everyone buckled and comfy back there?" Captain Eric Curry asked. He and Lieutenant James Rodriguez were piloting the Blackhawk back to the Telluride airfield.

"Yeah, where find, sir." The big medic answered after surveying everyone. Shauna Johnson was a large, raw-boned woman with coal-black hair, a big sense of humor and an easy smile. But now she was all business attending to her patient, Alice Thompson. She could tell that Alice was clearly traumatized. Alice was breathing rapidly trying to regurgitate the events of the last few days. She was amazed that Alice made it to the landing site.

How did she know where to go? And then there was her physical condition. Outside of a few cuts and bruises and covered with soot, Alice looked to be in pretty good shape. She was still coughing from the smoke she inhaled, obviously from the cabin fire she talked about. Shauna had already instructed the lieutenant to call the sheriff's office and report that Alice's husband, Frank Thompson, had left their cabin over two days ago trying to make his way to Telluride. Shauna turned back to Alice and instructed her to purge her lungs as best she could and then she would be putting her on oxygen. She had already checked her pulse and blood pressure and they were understandably high. However, she was more concerned about Alice's emotional and mental state.

The poor lady had gone through a lot in the last three weeks: the fire, cougar attack, isolation with food and fuel supplies running low, freezing from the cold and not knowing if her husband was okay. As Shauna studied Alice, her eyes looked almost haunted as if she knew something that couldn't be explained. She kept asking about Frank and the medic kept reassuring her that he would be found soon.

"They have one mountain rescue ground crew looking for him right now and another one is on their way."

"What about planes and helicopters... Why can't we use them to help search for Frank?" Alice asked.

"We can't do much in the dark because it poses too many hazards for air search. If our ground crews don't find him air rescue and search will be up at first light. Don't worry, we'll find him." She wasn't about to tell her of the approaching Derecho.

Alice wasn't so sure. *The weather had turned for the worse and who knows what it will be like tomorrow morning*, she thought. She tried to get her mind off the events of the last few days. She was dead tired, and breathing slowly and evenly through the oxygen aspirator helped her to relax. Alice turned to the back of the helicopter to make sure that the hunters were okay before she drifted to the other side of light.

Clyde Easton and Leroy Hazelton were sitting in the back with Earl Garvey. They hadn't spoken to each other since buckling up. All three were bone tired and in their own worlds thinking about what had happened over the last few hours and the mystery surrounding the wolf's tracks. As Clyde was nodding off he saw himself as a boy having dreams about a large gray wolf.

The visions that he had experienced were so vivid and intense that his parents had decided to send him to a psychiatrist. The nightmares had terrified him. Why was the wolf stalking him? The huge creature had leered at him night after night, saliva dripping from his fangs, threatening to overwhelm his subconscious. He thought the wolf had been sent to harm him and others. *Could his dreams be connected to the others and could he communicate to them to warn them about the wolf?* He thought. Also, he had often wondered if the wolf was a connection to his past life or an open door to his future. He had been sure that his dreams were connected to other people or perhaps the wolf. Maybe the brilliant blue eyes of the creature had been empowering him to warn others despite the wolf's intentions. *Can wolves dream and connect?* It had seemed contrary to his belief, but he did get the distinct feeling that all good had left the night run and had been replaced by evil. And he had thought somehow it wasn't the wolf's fault–something had happened.

The psychiatrist had quoted Freud, Jung and Darwin to him and had explained how the evolution of dreams parallels that of man. He went on to say as mankind progresses and evolves so do his dreams. In his eyes, groups of people would eventually connect through their dreams and control other groups, similar to propaganda except on a metaphysical level and this progression would continue until all of society would become interdependent.

Clyde remembered that his parents had pulled him out of therapy after six sessions–they had said something about how he didn't need counseling and that the dreams would eventually pass. They had been right and if the truth were to be told, his parents had suspected the psychiatrist was trying to explain his own theories to the young Easton and had shown no regard for his well-being. It took him some years before he had realized the favor his parents had done, and that they had discontinued the therapy sessions after finding the good doctor wanted to prescribe antipsychotic medication for their son. He did recall that the wolf's name in his dreams was Rollo, but he wasn't sure if the creature left any tracks. A chill ran over him. Here he was twenty years later encountering something that could be connected to his dreams.

Captain Curry's voice floated over the intercom. "Folks, buckle tight and stow any loose containers." He momentarily paused to confer with his copilot and then continued. "As you know the flight has been rough so don't expect any better with the landing."

The big medic was troubled about what she had heard from Alice. There weren't any hunters helping her as she had said, but how did she make it out on her own? The improbability of Alice knowing where the landing site was and then making it there from the cabin was almost beyond belief. *There has to be more to this story,* Shauna thought. The medic then reached over to wake Alice and helped her tighten her seat restraint and told her that they were about to land.

THIRTY-THREE

Finding Frank

The radio crackled. "Art, you there?" Abe asked. "Yeah, go ahead," Art said.

"Steve and I just got back to the rigs."

"Did you find anything–any tracks, tread marks or evidence of a person or persons traveling along the snowfield?" Art asked.

Abe looked at Steve before answering. "No, nothing at all, just more boulders, uprooted trees and snow."

"Abe, we just received more information from the captain. The helo has collected Alice Thompson and she is okay. Although it appears the Thompson's cabin has burnt to the ground. Her husband, Frank had left the cabin over two days ago and is trying to make his way to town. Also, three of the hunters are in the chopper with Alice. Jim Hazelton and Umberto Sanches decided to stay behind. We don't know why, except that they wanted to look for tracks behind the cabin. The storm will hit soon and I hope Jim and Umberto take cover because the weather service fears that a Derecho is coming with straight line winds over 100 mph. We all need to take cover soon. Right now we are halfway between the lake and the main road and we're still finding tread marks and they appear to be more distinct in some areas."

"So, it looks like you're getting closer to Frank?"

"I believe so, but we need to move fast, cause the snow is obliterating his tracks."

"What are your instructions, boss?" Abe asked.

"Head back to town. We have already turned back two other rescue teams coming up the mountain because of the storm and the impending Derecho." Doc looked at Art and shook his head. He couldn't hear much because of the blasted wind, but he heard the part about the storm.

"Winds could hit 100 miles per hour up here on the mountain?" Doc exclaimed.

"Yeah, that's what I'm afraid of. If we don't find Frank soon and get out of here we could all be in trouble, Doc."

"I hear you, but don't the other two hunters have their own helo coming tomorrow morning?" Doc asked.

"They do, but the storm may get in the way." Art turned back to the radio and could hear Abe telling Steve to turn the furnace down. "Abe you still there?"

"Yeah, you know they may not get out tomorrow."

"How well I know." Art replied. "These guys better be prepared and I'm sure they know that the weather can change on a dime up here. I know one of them by reputation. Jim Hazelton is clear up the food chain for hunting guides."

"Well, it must've been damn important to stay on the mountain. That's all I can say."

"It is for them—they're Big Horn hunting." Art said.

"They could put a lot of people in jeopardy if they can't get out."

"That's for sure. Just a minute, Abe, I think Olaf has found something. I'll radio you back for more information." Art cut the connection.

Olaf came lumbering up the hill in his snowshoes waving at the men. He seemed agitated and excited all at the same time. "What is it?" Art yelled.

"There's a crevasse at the bottom of the hill and I found an orange hair band tied to the end of a pole sticking out of the snow ten feet beyond the edge."

Art looked at Doc and Angel and said, "What are we waiting for?"

Oly held up his hand. "Now wait a minute, we need to be careful. There's a crevasse down there and I don't know how large or deep it is. Did any of you bring crampons?"

The group shook their heads. Art knew when to relinquish authority and this was one of those times. Olaf continued. "Since I'm the only one that has ice equipment, I'll be the outside guy on this operation. Now I only want two of us down there at a time and we need to tie off. Understand?" The men nodded.

Art knew about Oly's background. He was a certified mountain and ice climber who had scaled many of the Northwest's mountain peaks numerous times that included Hood, Rainier, Adams, and Baker. He had also climbed Whitney in California and McKinley in Alaska. In his younger years you could also add K2 and Everest to his resume. But for some reason he had never climbed any of the Fourteens in his home state, Colorado. Art surmised since he was up here in the mountains anyway doing mountain rescue, what was the difference?

The men tied themselves off with Olaf at the point–closest to the crevasse. Art and Doc anchored from the top of the hill while Angel and Olaf made their way down to the orange marker in the snow. Once down the two men looked around and could see deep gouge marks in the snow with rope laying across a Colorado blue spruce straddling the crevasse.

"What do we have here?" Olaf said. He looked closely at the gouge marks and the rope in front of him. He didn't see the familiar claw marks of crampons in the snow. "If I didn't know any better it looks like someone fell in and somehow was able to climb out without sharkies." Oly took his probe, extended it and turned on the infrared thermal imaging system. The technology not only registered the heat of an object but also gave an outline of an object up to one hundred feet away, and indicated the depth of the target. The equipment wasn't State issued and Olaf had paid a handsome sum for the gear, but it was well worth the money.

He was anxious to try it out and knew this would be one of the tools used in the future for mountain rescue units. The benefits were undeniable–locating people and animals very quickly under life and death situations. The only drawback he could see was the cost, but that would come down in time once the technology became more common. It wasn't long before the small screen showed a human form ten feet south of the orange hair band and six inches below the snow's surface. The two men rushed to the spot, snapped open their survival shovels and began to dig, being careful to shovel around the figure. Olaf turned to the two men anchoring them on the top of the short hill and yelled. "We have Frank Thompson and I believe he's still alive. Slide down the Sked rescue unit."

"You want us down there?" Art yelled.

"No, stay put–I'm not sure how stable the crevasse is. Did you bring a thermal blanket?" Olaf asked.

"Sure did." Art replied.

"Slide it down with the stretcher." Olaf slid off his right glove and placed two fingers on Frank's carotid artery and took his pulse. It was weak, about forty-five beats per minute. His breathing was shallow and his lips were turning blue. By now Angel had detached the Sked and blanket from the line and was tugging it over to Olaf.

"How is he?"

"Not good. He's suffering from hyperthermia. He has frostbite and his heart rate is in the forties."

"Can we move him?" Angel asked.

"Not far." Olaf turned to Frank again. "We're going to get you out of here so hold on big fellow." He wasn't sure if Frank could hear, but he had to let him know that they would do their best to save his life. Olaf yelled up the hill to Art. "This guy is in bad condition and we shouldn't move him too far."

"We can't get him to the junction? Art asked.

Olaf shook his head. "Fraid not. Look around you, Art. The snow is coming harder than ever and we need cover for this guy and for us all, now. We passed a small embankment fifty yards up the hill behind us. I want you and Doc to build a snow cave there- we'll have to wait out the storm."

Art now was worried. The storm had intensified in the last half hour and air rescue was probably out of the question. He radioed his boss and updated the captain on their present situation and asked about air rescue and the other three units making their way back to town.

Jason Whitfield paused for a long moment. "Art, I just received the latest forecast from the National Weather Service out of Denver.

The storm will intensify with blustery winds coming out of the northwest. They think it'll be a rare winter Derecho moving very hard and fast to the southeast. They said snowfall will be heavy with falling temperatures, and lightning strikes but the storm should be over by mid-day tomorrow. The other three mountain rescue units are about an hour out and will make it in. Can Mr. Thompson be taken quickly to the last rescue unit coming off the mountain?"

"No Olaf said he shouldn't be moved. Frank's in critical condition and needs to be airlifted."

"Art, we can't get you out right now. It won't be long before anyone will be moving anywhere on the mountain. All civil and military air transportation will be closing down in the area shortly until this monster passes."

"That bad, huh?" Art asked.

"Don't know yet for sure, but I wouldn't want to be stuck out in the open when this hits. You get crackin' and build a deep snow cave and we'll get you out tomorrow afternoon. You have enough food and supplies?" Jason asked.

"Yeah, we'll make it. What about Abe and Steve and the other mountain rescue unit?" Art asked.

"Again, as you know, everyone should be getting off the mountain while they can. I just pray to God those two other hunters hunker down and ride it out. Need to go."

The sat connection went dead. Art immediately radioed Abe and updated him on the situation and instructions he received from the captain. He was worried. As he and Doc trudged up the hill to build a snow cave, he was thinking if he had ever been in a Derecho. To his knowledge he couldn't recall–he would've known. He didn't know much about them because of their rarity, especially in winter but he knew they were nasty–damn nasty.

The huge gray creature surveyed the scene from behind a small grove of aspen trees. He was hoping his friend was okay. He would get closer but wasn't sure if they could see him and his instincts told him to be cautious. He would stay for a while and then check on him later–he had other business to attend.

THIRTY-FOUR

The Landing

The helo came in cautiously with Captain Curry feathering the controls. The Blackhawk swayed from side to side and almost stalled from the powerful wind shear caused by the storm. *This was going to be trial by fire,* he thought. The ride in was rough with poor visibility due to the rising snowstorm and the blustery winds didn't help either. Both he and the Lieutenant had their hands full. If they had waited another fifteen minutes they probably wouldn't have made it. *Thank God for instruments,* he thought. Ordinarily, the flight would have taken only fifteen minutes to the airfield from the landing site, but because of the conditions it had taken over thirty minutes. They were constantly buffeted by strong lateral winds coming from the northwest ahead of the storm front and at times he had to maneuver around strong downdrafts and snow squalls. The bird had a 19,000-foot ceiling, but under these conditions it was far less and he had to fly near whatever ceiling the storm gave him to avoid some of the turbulence.

After the chopper landed, Shauna Johnson, the medic accompanied Alice with the paramedics to the waiting ambulance and said her goodbyes. She knew that the ordeal wasn't over for Alice, but at least the captain gave her good news, during the flight, that her husband had been found. She still wondered what Alice was talking about. During the flight, Alice kept looking back to the bulkhead and questioning if the hunters were okay. Of course, they were in her mind. Perhaps it was the medication she gave her. She couldn't understand what Alice was saying, and why she was saying it.

After Alice was whisked away to Telluride Medical Center the flight crew including the crew chief met with Sheriff Whitfield at the county's administration building. Captain Whitfield wanted to know firsthand what the weather conditions were like because he still had two hunters on the loose out in the wilderness, and he had especially wanted to hear what Alice had told Shauna Johnson about the other three hunters. Maybe there was a clue as to where Hazelton and Sanches were heading. After the briefing, the sheriff wasn't any closer than he was before with the hunters. In fact, the mystery grew as to how Alice knew where the landing site was and how she ever made it out in her condition. He knew that Alice thought she was found by the five hunters and two of them stayed behind. Strike this. As far as his teams, the sheriff knew he made the right decision to pull them off the mountain.

THIRTY-FIVE

Telluride Regional
Medical Center

Alice was wheeled into the emergency room. The bright lights hurt her eyes. She was starving and asked one of the orderlies for some food. She hadn't had a decent meal in a long time, but she felt guilty asking because she was thinking of her husband out in the wilderness with very little nourishment for the last few days. Even though her husband had been found she really didn't know what shape he was in and hoped he was okay. She loved him very much and missed him. After the orderly had said no to food, he wheeled her into a private room off the emergency room vestibule and left her to her own thoughts. *She was sure glad the hunters found her when they did or she would have been a goner for sure,* she thought. Without their help in the helicopter she would have never made it here. What was the name of the lead hunter, she pondered. *Jim Hazelton?* She wondered. After awhile a handsome male nurse came in and did triage on her by taking her vitals, drew blood samples and hooked her to an IV. She was extremely dehydrated. Alice looked up to a pair of brown, soulful eyes and asked, "Any word on my husband yet?"

The nurse paused for a moment and then asked, "Is your husband Frank Thompson?"

"Yes." Alice said, as concern flashed across her face. "Is he okay?"

"I'll have to check. The last information we received was that he was found by a mountain rescue team."

"I know, but is he ok?" Alice asked. "How soon will he be in Telluride?"

"I don't know, mam. Like I said I'll have to check. And what about the hunters," she inquired. Raphael de Silva gave Alice a strange look with his muddy eyes, heavy with dread and confusion knowing what was coming. "I don't know about any hunters, mam, I'll have to check on that too." He knew that Frank was coming in, but he didn't recall hearing about any hunters. de Silva wasn't a God-fearing man anymore. He had seen too much in this world and his vision had been altered from that of when he was a child. But he would pray for her husband's safe return, and also the hunters. He knew that people could lose their lives in winter conditions like these and he sure wasn't going to tell her about the approaching Derecho. "Is there anything else you need before I go, perhaps another blanket?"

"No, I'm fine. Just let me know when you find anymore information about my husband."

"I will, mam, and one of the ER docs will be in shortly." Raphael left to attend to other duties. He hoped this wasn't going to be a busy shift, but with a Derecho approaching he wasn't sure. *And what about the hunters,* he thought again.

THIRTY-SIX

Flashover

While waiting for the ER doc, Alice, again thought about the hunters that were in the back of the helo. *Strange the nurse didn't know about them,* she thought. After Alice saw Clyde, Earl, and Leroy exit the helo she somehow knew they were headed to the New Sheridan Hotel in the downtown district. *Maybe that's why the nurse didn't know about them,* she thought.

Her mind was really working on overtime now as she imagined what it was like for the three hunters. The script was playing full line now as if someone or something was controlling the scene. As she played it out in her mind she could see that the hotel was only a short distance from the airport. It wasn't fancy but it was decent and had a good restaurant and bar. All five hunters already had reservations tomorrow, but not for tonight. The shuttle driver called ahead and the three hunters were in luck. They all had stayed there two days before leaving on the Bighorn hunt and left some of their gear in the hotel's ski lockers. They knew that an unusual storm was heading their way and wanted to be safely ensconced before it arrived. They were also worried about Jim and Humberto, but knew they were seasoned hunters and survivalists and could withstand almost anything. *If only they knew,* Alice thought.

After checking in all three gathered in Earl's room before heading to the bar. Even though Earl had turned up the heat all three were freezing. The cold penetrated the room turning the air frosty. Their hands and faces were white and their eyebrows icy. As Earl turned to the others to speak, a flash bolted out of nowhere and catapulted the hunters to the high valley a short way from Davidson Point. Alice caught her breath as she realized they were struggling to make sense of it all. Earl finally asked, "What the hell just happened? You guys look horrible. You're full of ice and you haven't taken your coats off yet."

Leroy looked to Clyde to take the lead since he was totally bewildered and his teeth were chattering so severely that he could barely speak. He felt as though he was frozen in time and space between two worlds: the one he was standing in, the other born elsewhere. The world borne of ice, snow and pain could not be denied; flashing in stuttered fragments, one by one, the room's ceiling, walls and floor fell away as Alice looked on in horror. The warm cozy world of comforting thoughts colored gone was now replaced by the harsh reality of where they were. The wind howled around them in raging currents like torrents in a river gone to flooding. Clyde, yelling at the top of his lungs struggled to be heard over the shrieking storm. The Derecho was upon them. "We need to take cover and fast–we won't last another fifteen minutes out here."

"But what happened to the hotel, and the town? Earl asked as shock rode the ridges of his frozen brows. Alice could clearly see Earl's face etched in ice, but how?

"I don't know. I only know we are going to freeze to death if we don't get moving." Clyde pointed to the west. It was almost a futile attempt in the blinding snow, but he had to try. "We need to dig a snow cave in the embankment and ride this monster out." He knew the winds were driving the wind chill to incredibly low temperatures and they had to hurry.

As they struggled on their snowshoes, trudging to the west bank, Leroy slowed and finally stopped. He was unable to go on. With all his strength and will slipping away he didn't care anymore, nor did he bother to yell. To Alice's amazement he crumpled to the snow with his face toward the wind and hands at his side, hoping the black curtain of death in the white wilderness would come and find him soon. He hoped his dad, wherever he was, would make it out. As blackness and cold descended upon him his thoughts faded to oblivion. Cold didn't seem to bother him anymore as the wind died around him. Everything died around him including himself. Alice could feel the chill of death surround her as she took a seat aboard the train of clairvoyance.

The void was falling on everything including Clyde and Earl as they neared the embankment. Earl turned back to check on Leroy, but he wasn't there not even his shadow. He yelled, but it was no use competing against the raging storm. The wind was so loud he couldn't even hear himself think. He couldn't feel anything and as he looked around he couldn't see anything not even Clyde; his sight was now seeing nothing but white.

By the time Clyde reached the hillside he was exhausted. He was young and a big man, but the storm had taken its toll. He was numb through and through and had trouble reaching for his snow shovel. It was in his backpack, but it seemed like forever maneuvering his back sack to the ground. *Did Colorado have hurricanes*, he thought. Pellets of ice glistening in the twilight like silver streams riding the currents of air, needlelike in their appearance, were assaulting his face as he turned back to yell at Earl and Leroy. Alice already knew that they weren't there in the white silvery veil of ice and snow. They were now ripped from the tapestry of life and Alice could see their faces fading away like a sunset frozen in space and time. The Derecho was at full force now, racing from the northwest to the southeast. At this elevation wind gusts were approaching one hundred miles per hour and wind chills were plummeting to ninety below zero, and total darkness was now descending like a veil of death. It didn't matter anymore. Clyde's face and eyes were so blistered from the onslaught he couldn't see anyway. As he tried to snap open the blade to the shovel's handle he was thinking how could this be. One moment they were standing in Earl's room, the next, stepping through the portrait into a maelstrom. *Was it a trick of the mind, or a dream? Was he delusional? And where did it begin? Was it at the hotel or perhaps at the cabin? Was the helicopter trip real or did he imagine it?* The last thing Clyde remembered was the wolf tracks and so did Alice.

THIRTY-SEVEN

Rollo

T he gray wolf could sense danger ahead as he approached the creek bed where the splitting took place eight months ago.

Even though the creek was now frozen over, he was sure this was where the incident had happened. His instincts told him this was a terrible place but he had to know why. The entity that had emerged from the creek bed that day had forever haunted him, linking his instincts filled with dread. It was now Rollo's calling to face the truth. Was it his doppelgänger or was it totally apart from him–some alien force frequenting his dreams? And what of the hunters and the couple? How was he able to know and connect with them? Was he communicating with them perhaps controlling them? Maybe the entity was orchestrating and controlling the dreams between him and the hunters and the couple. He had to know. Otherwise, he felt that he would never be accepted back into his old pack. He missed his mate and longed for the comfort that only she could provide.

It was now colder with snow, blowing in white curtains forming ice crystals on Rollo's fur as he stepped down the embankment to the creek bed. The wind intensified as the Derecho moved closer. He sniffed the frozen ground, looking for clues along the creek's edge–anything that would help find who he was. The scent of the struggle was long gone and the only thing he found was more snow and ice. He looked around and behind for tracks fresh or otherwise and found nothing. No one had been here, probably since winter had set in. He was about to leave when an unholy sound rolled above his head in the white dusk.

He froze, listening intently as the howl seemed to grow louder, gradually changing to a growl. Was it the wind? No. It was now nearer when he swung his head back to look across the frozen creek. To his horror, a vision of the creature arose from the ice in the middle of the creek. The gossamer edges of the apparition grew in size as it took shape. It seemed to shimmer, dancing within the white curtain of falling snow, fading in and out to the rhythm of the wind. Its fur was glistening with silver iridescence as if standing in full sunlight. The creature beckoned Rollo to come closer as lightning struck and thunder clapped from the snow- laden clouds. Rollo, spooked from the storm and the vision looked around again, hoping for help–anything since his instincts were failing him. He stepped gingerly on to the ice, testing it. Looking again at the ghost a bolt of lightning struck behind the creature, lighting everything around them and momentarily blinding him. When his vision returned the specter was now standing beside him on the ice looking at him. Rollo turned and bolted up the embankment terrified of the entity and the storm. As the weather front unleashed its fury with trees shaking and bending, Rollo ran for all he was worth. He didn't know where he was going–just away from the phantom. Running to the top of the hill where he and the bear had been fighting he suddenly stopped.

The entity was waiting for him. He was disappointed in the wolf's reaction to him. He wasn't in a threatening posture; he was here to help. Coming from the netherworld he understood Rollo's predicament. Caught between two worlds in the valley of shadows, Rollo didn't understand that he was already dead from the bear attack. He was merely a pawn–a means to an end that provided a connection to the childhood dreams of the couple and the hunters. He wasn't in control, and the sooner that Rollo understood his place in all of this, the sooner he could move on to his afterlife. The creature was growing impatient for his bet to arrive–he needed to get back to his friend. The wager was if he could help Rollo and Frank, he could move on to another place in time or forever be stuck in the wasteland, floating on the river Styx somewhere between the world of the living and the dead.

Rollo could see the gray-silver beast standing alone and facing him at the spot where he and the black bear started their dance of death down the incline. He was afraid of his doppelgänger not knowing what to do next. He sensed it was the same with Charlie and the pack not knowing what the beta was going to do. Somewhere between instinct and reason he could see the irony of it all. The creature was motioning for him to come closer and gather his knowledge. Halfway up the long hill the pull of the creature became stronger, beckoning Rollo to continue. As he advanced a god awful sound sprang from the apparition's throat, riding the currents it distorted Rollo's hearing. He was terrified at what was coming, but he had to find out. His vision blurring against the blinding snow, he thought he saw the creature move from side-to-side, but really wasn't moving at all. It's translucent, needle-like fur glistening in the snowstorm like some "Fata Morgana" in the desert wavering in the heat, stacking and restacking. Was the entity there? The prism-like vision kept changing further confusing and blinding him with fear as the howl of the wind increased in intensity, matching the creature's sound. Terror now replacing fear in the seat of instinct, riding the tails of madness, Rollo turned and bolted down the hill.

The creature with its eye shine from the fires of hell drove Rollo on encasing him in his folly. The wolf was now at full stride rushing down the hill, racing to his destiny. The last thing he saw before crossing the river Styx into the world of the dead was a pair of sky blue eyes urging him on. The same rock that had killed the bear had now killed Rollo. The scales of life and death had now been balanced at least for Rollo and the entity. The creature could now help Frank and finish his business before moving on.

THIRTY-EIGHT

Derecho

At the top of the hill Art and Doc unsnapped their snow shovels, extended the handles and began the arduous task of digging a snow cave. They knew this monster of a storm was upon them and they had to shovel fast. It was fall dark now and the winds were ferocious coming out of the northwest, roaring like a freight train gone out of control. They tried to keep their backs to the onslaught; it felt like slivers of steel. The temperature had fallen so rapidly in the last hour or so that the snow had coalesced into ice pellets bringing the pain. The groves of Aspens that grew at this elevation were now their enemy, slinging wooden arrows driven by the Derecho. Even though Art couldn't see more than a few feet around him he knew the air was filled with debris–he could feel it. He turned and squinted through his goggles to check on Angel and Olaf and only could see a wall of white. Visibility was now near zero and he felt disoriented and claustrophobic. Cold was becoming their enemy the longer they were exposed to the elements.

"Let's hurry, Doc. Olaf and Angel will be here soon with Mr. Thompson and I want this thing done."

"You don't have to tell me–I'm freezing my butt off."

"Yeah, the wind is slicing through me like butter–never seen anything like it." As the two men continued to dig, Angel and Olaf struggled with Frank pulling the Sked up the hill. Frank Thompson was a big man with a lot of heft and it took all the might the two men could muster, especially in these conditions.

Olaf was a big man himself, burly and strong, but without crampons he doubted if it wouldn't have mattered. His muscles ached as they trudged on. Without snowshoes on every step he took, Olaf sunk deep into the snow. He had no choice. Even though the trek to where Doc and Art were digging was not far the slope was steep and icy. With both of them in snowshoes they wouldn't have made it. Even the newer ultra-light composite snowshoes with metal teeth would have been no match for the slippery slope they were on.

As they approached the other men, at least by his best estimates, Olaf yelled out. After his third try he thought he heard a reply from either Art or Doc, but couldn't be sure because of the howling wind. He continued up the hill with Angel behind him and Frank trailing in the Sked. Hearing another voice to his left, disembodied in its utterance Olaf wondered if it wasn't his imagination. He looked behind him and motioned Angel to stop. His friend was only five feet away tethered to the same climbing line, but it was difficult to see him. As he cleared his goggles and brought up the brightly lit GPS screen to his eyes he could see that they were on track and in the general area where Art and Doc should be digging. If he had known beforehand about finding Frank at this location, he could've marked and entered the exact area for the snow cave on the GPS. It would have made it much easier to find them. But with visibility near zero and the wind driving the snow and ice in torrents, he was now worried he wouldn't find them. Then it happened. A sound different from the wind rifled over the white wilderness almost on top of him. It was them. Lounging forward he tripped over Art as he was digging. "Thank God we found you," Olaf shouted.

Art turned to face his friend and helped him back to his feet. "Yeah, I was worried that you and Angel were lost. You can't see past your hand in this madness."

Olaf looked past Art and could see the snow cave was nearly finished. "Nice job, buddy," Olaf said as Art and Doc grabbed the climbing rope to haul Angel and the Sked to the snow cave's opening. As Angel came into view, Doc smiled and said, "It's about time."

With great effort the men dragged the Sked into the snow cave. While Art and Doc continued to dig out the enclosure, Angel and Olaf snapped open more glow sticks and attended to Frank. His breathing was still shallow but at least he was alive. Olaf looked at his watch and figured they had between sixteen to twenty hours before life flight arrived, and that's if the storm subsided. He hoped that Frank would make it, but now first things first. He cracked open some green heat canisters, shook them, and placed them around the snow enclosure and a few next to Frank. It was a much-needed upgrade over Sterno–quicker, hotter and cleaner. He moved outside and planted the GPS locator beacon next to the entrance. By the time he walked back inside, Doc and Art were finished digging. The four men took turns keeping Frank warm, all wondering what the hell they got themselves into.

Art checked his watch with his hand-held LED light and saw that it was 6:00 pm. Between the helmet lights and the glow sticks there was sufficient light to see everyone. "Okay boys we sit and wait out this storm and hope the helo comes tomorrow morning. Let's double-check our inventory."

"I'm already ahead of you Art." Olaf had already gone through his backpack and coat pockets and laid everything next to the Sked. Everyone else went through their gear and mentally noted everything they had. Each person on the team had forty-pound SAR soft packs that contained cold weather gear, utensils, food, water and a host of other items to sustain them up to seventy-two hours. In addition, they carried extra medical supplies because of the nature of the rescue and the information they had already received. After the inventory check they turned their attention back to Frank Thompson. By now the temperature in the cave had risen to just above freezing from the body heat of its occupants and the green heat canisters. The outside entrance to the cave was facing away from the storm to allow for proper ventilation and to minimize wind chill. Each man worked quickly and efficiently as a team to revive Frank. After they built a secondary enclosure to trap some of the heat around Frank they placed more heat canisters nearby. This would enable his core temperature to rise even further. Olaf checked his vital signs again and found that his pulse was improving along with his temperature. After another thirty minutes, Frank began to stir and asked where he was.

"We found you, Frank, and you're now with the mountain rescue team." Art said as he reached over and tilted the water canteen gently to Frank's lips. "Just take a few sips big fella."

After Frank finished with the water, Doc handed some warm chicken broth to Angel. "Sip it slowly." Angel then mouthed to Olaf to check his feet again. Some of his toes were black with frostbite.

"Why am I burning up and how do you know my name?" Frank asked as he looked up to Angel.

"Slow down and just rest, Frank. You've been through a lot and your body is now adjusting to the temperature change and you will be in some discomfort for a while." Angel motioned again to Olaf to check his legs. He wanted to see if he was getting circulation. His clothes were fairly dry because of the extreme cold and dry conditions so they decided not to strip his clothes off, but rather work through his pants to massage his legs. The team already knew about his right arm being bitten and also discovered that he had some cracked ribs on his left side and bruising over a good portion of his body. Olaf nodded at Angel knowing now that Frank had fallen into the crevasse and somehow had climbed out. He also knew that Frank needed to be immersed in a water bath in a controlled environment to help regulate his core temperature, but they would have to make do. "We need you to drink more water," Olaf said. "It'll help hydrate you and regulate your temperature." As Frank sipped more water Art moved to the opening to check on the conditions. They were frightful. The snow or rather ice pellets were blowing totally horizontal as the wind pushed them ever faster. Art was staring at a white gossamer curtain and couldn't see beyond it, but he could certainly hear the roar of the wind. In all his life he had never seen conditions like this, but then again he had never been trapped high on a mountain in the middle of winter during a Derecho. Moving back, he could now see that Frank was regaining some of his color.

"How are you doing?" Art asked.

"I feel like hell and hurting all over, and how do you know my name?" Frank asked again. "And what about Alice is she okay?"

After taking in more broth and feeling a little better Olaf redressed the wound on his right arm. The team then told Frank about the circumstances that led them to him, and that Alice was airlifted from the cabin to Telluride Regional Medical Center.

They didn't want to upset him anymore than he was and kept the details to a minimum. There was no mention of a cabin fire.

Frank looked around at the group and asked again, "How is she?"

Art moved toward Frank and in an earnest voice said,

"She's a little shaken but she'll be fine. As soon as the helo arrives we'll be flying you there. Right now though we have to stay hunkered down because of the winter storm." Art looked around at the others before he spoke again. "Frank, I'm going to be honest with you. If we wouldn't have found you when we did, I don't believe you would have survived the storm."

"How bad am I?" Frank asked. "Nothing we can't handle, buddy."

"Is a helicopter coming?"

"Yes, and it'll be here as soon as it can get through." Art looked at his watch. "It's a fast-moving storm so we should be out of here in about twelve hours." Art wasn't so sure. It could be much longer but he didn't want to say anything to alarm Frank.

"You need to get some rest now—conserve your strength." Olaf took his temperature and pulse again. His pulse was near normal now but his core temperature was still below normal—in the low nineties, but much better than it had been. Frank started to mumble something about his ordeal but eventually drifted off. Even though he was still in some pain the sedative he had received took hold and calmed his nerves. It wasn't long before he was dreaming about the wolf with the sky blue eyes.

THIRTY-NINE

Rendezvous Point

T he snow and ice pellets driven by ferocious winds intensified the further south Jim and Humberto walked. Dusk had already paid its visit an hour ago and the men had to rely on their GPS to keep them heading in the right direction. Jim thought the wind was gusting to over fifty miles per hour now with wind chill approaching negative forty below. Even though they were skilled outdoorsmen and appropriately dressed they would have to dig in soon. *Was it his imagination or was he getting colder by the minute*, he thought. They would never make it to Davidson Point in these conditions. He tapped Bert on the shoulder, no use to yell over the wind. When Bert turned toward him, Jim pointed to the west side of the valley. Humberto nodded and both men headed to the embankment. They needed to build a snow cave and wait out this monster. At this elevation the valley afforded scent protection from the wind. Aspens and spruce were far and few between.

As they changed direction, Jim thought about the disappearing wolf tracks and the huge gray wolf in his childhood dreams–the one with the sky blue eyes. A chill came over him, not from the cold but the thought that this wolf could be one and the same. *Was there a connection?* He wasn't sure, but why did it keep entering his mind? What was it about the wolf in his dreams; something didn't add up? He really never gave it much thought until he saw the disappearing tracks in the snow at the burnt out cabin and the landing site. Now as he and Humberto were struggling to stay alive it came around the bend in a blinding flash of recognition. It was Charlie all along and it had always been Charlie the little omega. With his strength ebbing because of the conditions he was now forced to face his fears and shortcomings or be forever lost in the doldrums of time. His son, Leroy came into focus. Leroy and Charlie, Charlie and Leroy. *Were they one and the same*, he thought. He was always pushing his son aside because he didn't think he measured up. Always shoving him beyond his capabilities and never giving him any slack, Jim now knew that his son would probably never forgive him, just like Charlie would never forgive Rollo, especially since this had been going on for so long. He was the alpha wolf the one with the sky blue eyes, always translucent in nature and personality, and always standing at the edge waiting for his son to catch up. He knew that his son would never equal him, not in his ways. Leroy was cut from a different strand of cloth. One was made of steel; the other of cotton. He knew his son could never follow in his footsteps. How could he? His tracks kept disappearing in life just like the wolf's tracks kept disappearing in the snow. He wondered if wolves had relationships like humans and he was sure that they did. After all, they were social creatures and ran in packs. And just like humans they interacted with their families. He already found the alpha or rather his tracks and he was sure the little omega, Charlie, was somewhere on the mountainside just like his son.

Jim peered into the white wilderness trying to see where Humberto was. He was nowhere in site. He yelled into the maelstrom hoping for his voice to reach him, but he knew it would be to no avail. The wind was now shrieking as a huge gust swept him off his feet. He landed hard, face first in the snow with his fists pounding the icy morass in frustration. He stopped moving thinking about what had happened. He must have been so caught up in his thoughts that he became disoriented and lost his way. He reached for his GPS but his arms and hands wouldn't move. He tried getting to his knees but another gust knocked him over. The icy needles punched him as his breath caught in his throat. With his face full of ice and snow, he tried again to get to his knees but couldn't. Like a voracious animal the wind worked itself into the smallest gaps in his clothing applying its biting grip. His thoughts were coming in flashes now as he flailed at the snow trying to dig a snow cave. As he drifted toward the black curtain of death his thoughts turned again to the wolf. A strange presence of serenity came over him. The strings of life pulled harder the closer he got to death. *Is he seeing his life flash before him or is he merely a marionette being controlled by a puppeteer?* He thought. Perhaps the wolf was his puppeteer.

FORTY

Snow Cave

The team didn't get much sleep throughout the night–they were too amped. Besides the infernal wind was driving everyone nearly crazy. The sounds erupting from the snow cave's mouth ran the gamut from wailing banshees to howling wolves as the Derecho bounced off the mountain peaks. Taking turns watching and caring for Frank Thompson benefited not only Frank but also the team knowing that they had done a good job. Frank was somewhat responsive now but he seemed to be in more pain. Olaf knew that coming out of a lethargic state of hyperthermia would pose other challenges for them and for Frank. But without a controlled environment they would hope for the best with the supplies and equipment they had. It was now 10 hours and the storm seemed to be subsiding. Art was again on his satellite phone trying to reach Captain Whitfield while the others were going through their MRE's. The Meal Ready-To-Eat was a big improvement over the canned meals of the 80s. During the height of the storm the team had lost all communication with the command center and were cut off from the outside world.

"Captain, you there?" Art asked again. He had been trying to get through for the past ten minutes and the only thing that greeted him was static.

From the other end Jason Whitfield was hearing a series of high-pitched squeals. and an occasional low rumble interspersed with disembodied voices from the netherworld or so it seemed. Finally… "Captain, this is Art, can you hear me sir?"

"Loud and clear sergeant–how are you and the team doing?" Jason asked.

"We're okay."

Jason looked around the command center and he could see the relief on his team's faces. "How is our guest doing, Art?"

"Okay, sir. I'll put Olaf on the line since he can explain Frank's medical condition better than I." Frank turned to his friend and a short discussion ensued before he handed over the iridium satellite transceiver.

"Captain, Olaf here."

Jason ignored the pleasantries and went straight to the question. "How is Frank Thompson doing?"

"He's still in critical condition but holding his own. His core temperature has risen to the mid-nineties and he has gained most of his color back. His feet and some of his fingers are black with frostbite and I'm not sure if he will regain function in those areas."

"Will he be stable for the next few hours?"

"I think so. But he also has three cracked ribs from a fall into a crevasse; claw marks on his back and a wound on his right forearm that looks like it came from large canines. He's in bad shape, but one tough dude. He's been through a lot and needs better medical attention."

"Olaf, we're working on that and just as soon as the storm abates will get you out. Now, what about the wound on his forearm? Was he attacked by a wolf?"

"I don't know for sure. He's been drifting in and out of consciousness since we revived him. But in one of his more lucid moments he did mention being attacked by a wolf and then he said the strangest thing."

"What's that?" The captain asked.

"He said that a wolf-like creature with sky blue eyes suddenly appeared and chased away the other wolf. And when I questioned him further he said it looked like an apparition with needle like fur and the creature's prints appeared to disappear in the snow."

"What do you mean by 'prints disappearing in the snow?" Jason asked.

"Sir, he said that he had seen the creature two or three times while making his way down the mountain and each time he saw the wolf-like apparition his prints would disappear as he ran off.

Frank thinks the entity was trying to help him. Beyond that I couldn't get much more out of him."

"A mysterious creature with sky blue eyes and disappearing prints? He's probably hallucinating from the extreme cold and what he's been through"

"I agree. Oh one other thing, he was very adamant about the attack and he described his protector in great detail. Not only from the standpoint of the attack, but he also indicated that the creature helped him out of the crevasse. His story is just amazing and I'm sure that we will have to investigate this further."

"Yes we will. Olaf, good job in finding Mr. Thompson and keeping him stable. Now I need to speak with Art again."

"Thanks, but what about the helo, sir?"

"That's why I need to talk to Art … update him with the latest information." Jason was getting a little impatient with Olaf.

He knew he was an experienced mountaineer, but sometimes he wanted too much of the limelight.

"Yeah, boss what's going on?" Art asked as he looked at Olaf after receiving the transceiver.

Again, Jason didn't waste any time. "First of all, Alice Thompson is now at Telluride Medical Center."

"How is she?" Art asked.

"She's a little banged up and dehydrated, and the medical staff said she was somewhat unresponsive at times, and mumbling about some hunters. I think she is still reliving her stay at the cabin and hasn't quite come to terms about her situation. And what I just heard from Olaf about a phantom wolf I'm now wondering what Alice saw including the hunters. Things just don't add up."

"You don't have to tell me, sir. Now about Alice will she be okay?" Art asked.

"All in all I think she'll be fine, but she is going to need time to process everything and some serious psychological counseling. It appears that she has really been traumatized by the whole thing

- who wouldn't be." Jason rubbed his dark stubble–he had been up for nearly forty-eight hours catching a few catnaps now and then. He looked at his team again and could see that they were just as perplexed as he was. He would have to chalk it up to hallucinations for the time being–what else could it be?

"I'll tell Frank that Alice is fine. Any word on the hunters?"

"No nothing yet. I just hope they are hunkered down somewhere." Jason knew if they got caught out in the open that it would probably be too late to dig in. He had already checked with NOAA about the conditions higher on the mountain and it wasn't pretty. With wind gusts over ninety miles per hour and temperatures at thirty below the wind chill would be in excess of eighty below zero. No one in the open would last more than a few minutes under these conditions.

"Well if Jim Hazelton's reputation holds true they are all dug in somewhere and waiting out this monster."

"Sure hope so, Art … sure hope so. Just a minute." The captain took the latest weather report from Sergeant Dan Hoffman and quickly read it. "Art, looks like we can get a bird up to you in about four hours. I see your GPS beacon signal is strong so the Guard shouldn't have any trouble finding it."

"Where will they land, sir?" Art asked.

"About a half a mile west of where you are. There's a wide spot between the slopes there. The team will make their way to your location and help everyone back to the helo. Art, is everyone okay besides Frank?"

"Yeah were in good shape and in good spirits, now that we have heard from you. What about the ground crews–did they make it back?"

"Yeah, Abe Silvers and the boys were pulled off in time. As a matter of fact Abe will be part of the mountain rescue team coming to you in about four hours. I'm sure you guys have a lot to talk about." The captain knew that his team and the mountain rescue teams worked closely together. They had to because of the work they did, especially in conditions like these. "Okay, buddy, hang in there. I'll be updating you on the hour, and if changes occur you'll be the first to know."

"Thanks, Captain." The connection went dead. Art knew that the Captain was under a lot of stress, they all were. He was particularly worried about the hunters. No one had heard from them for over five days. The Captain had said their helo ride was canceled because of the storm, and the company was unable to reach them. They could be stuck anywhere on the mountain.

FORTY-ONE

The Transfer

The big Sikorsky came in fast and hard, and feathered over the landing sight. The wind was still a handful for the bird and Captain Alicia Munson wanted to make sure she hit the mark. The target area was a little tight but the slope next door afforded her some protection from the wind. She had a lot of hours in the rotary wing, working for the Guard, but flying in this stuff was always treacherous. White billows of snow mushroomed below from its four-bladed rotors as the Blackhawk sat down in the snow. The mountain rescue team members and the medics were in a hurry. They wanted to get to Frank Thompson as soon as possible, get him to the chopper and then to Telluride Regional Medical Center. The wind was still a problem gusting to fifty miles per hour, causing near white-out conditions, but this is where their training paid off. They all knew if it wasn't for the emergency beacon placed at the mouth of the snow cave marking their location they would have never found them. Half a mile hike in these conditions felt more like five miles.

As the four men tethered themselves for the trip to the snow cave, the lead, Abe Silvers was amazed at the ferocity of the storm. Even though it had lessened considerably in the last hour or so he could feel the ice pellets assault his back–even through his gear. Looking ahead was like seeing a wall of white, except he was part of it. Looking back he couldn't see George Hawkinson, one of the medics. He could only see the climbing rope disappear into a cloud of white. He knew he was there because of the tug on the line. They were heading southeast from the bird and going downhill with the wind. He hated to think about the return trip in these conditions–going up hill and facing the wind. Even with high tech gear the trek to the snow cave took over an hour. After missing on the first approach he hit the beacon on the second try. The team found that the snow cave wasn't large enough to accommodate all four of them so the two newer members waited at the mouth of the cave while Abe and George went inside.

Stooping further to avoid the ceiling they inched along until they saw the other team members crowding around the Sked. Abe could tell they were ready to go, seeing all their gear packed and everything collected.

As George moved toward Olaf and Frank Thompson to get Frank's vitals, Abe talked to the other three men.

"How's Frank holding up?"

"He's holding his own." Olaf said.

"But we need to get him to TRMC as soon as we can." Doc cut in.

Abe peered at George. "Is he stable enough to move?"

"His vitals aren't what I would like, but we have no choice." George removed Frank's gloves, boots and socks and examined his hands first while Olaf pointed his high-intensity LED flashlight. George could see that two of his fingers on his right hand were multi-colored and turning black in places. His other hand looked pretty good, but some of his toes were another matter. They were blistered black and felt hard to the touch. "His fingers have frostnip, but some of his toes have frostbite, possibly third or fourth degree."

"Will he suffer any permanent damage?" Angel asked.

George looked directly at Angel and answered, "Don't know yet, it's too soon to tell. We'll know more after we get him to the hospital."

"Did you bring the gurney bubble?" Art asked.

"Sure did." George said. George Hawkinson was a large man like Abe and an excellent medic. As a young man, George saw a lot of action in the Gulf Wars with multiple tours. When he got back to

Colorado he advanced his medical training and joined the Mountain Rescue Unit in Telluride.

"Okay, I want everyone out except George and myself." Art looked at the others and motioned them to leave. "Once we get the bubble to the cave's opening you guys help us get him outside. Now let's go."

After most of the team had crawled to the entrance, George and Art were left with the delicate task of moving Frank from the Sked to the gurney bubble. There was a plastic liner on the interior of the Sked with short handles that made the job of moving Frank much easier. After the chore was completed they snapped the clear bubble in place. The gurney bubble was a relatively new piece of equipment that enabled mountain rescue members to transport critically injured people in adverse conditions. Once in place the hermetically sealed environment, inside the bubble, could be adjusted by anyone on the outside. In Frank's case the pressure and humidity were set to roughly equal to the outside environment while the air temperature was set to fifty degrees.

The medics didn't want to shock Frank's biosystems too severely, but rather to bring his environment slowly to room temperature, which would also aid in raising his core temperature. The process would take some time and the task would be completed at Telluride Regional Medical Center.

The team members were all tethered together because of the whiteout and it was slow going to the bird. The climb, uphill, was arduous and because of the wind the team traded positions often, seeking redress from the relentless assault of ice pellets and other debris. Abe was at point in front of the bubble paying strict attention to his GPS, and making sure that they were heading in the right direction toward the helo. He had no protection in front of him and with the outside air temperature close to thirty below with winds gusting to fifty miles per hour it was almost unbearable. Nonetheless the team trudged on at the corner of pain and cold. Under these conditions they all knew the captain would continue to run the chopper's twin engines and time was of the essence because of fuel concerns. Out of the curtain of white, twin high-intensity red beacons flashed in the gloom. The red against the white background was a beautiful vision to Abe and the rescue team. He turned toward the bubble and was about to say something and then thought better of it. No one could hear him anyway not over the roar of the wind. Two Guard members tethered to the chopper suddenly appeared out of the white to help the team aboard with their survivor. After everyone was in, and Mr. Thompson was secured and attended to and short introductions were made and everyone took their seats and secured themselves, the chopper prepared to lift off.

FORTY-TWO

Life Flight

The flight back was going to be rough. Captain Monson motioned to Lieutenant Rob McIvey as if to say are you ready? The rotors revved up and the twin engines went nearly to full power as the bird struggled for stability in the wind. After a short lift off the helo veered 135 degrees to come in line with its pre-arranged vectors and headed southeast toward Telluride. The chopper fought for stability as it swayed and pitched from the buffeting winds. As the captain and lieutenant feathered the controls of the big Blackhawk, the Guard and mountain rescue team remained quiet with solemn faces. The bird weaved itself through the declining storm like a boxer staggering from a knockout punch. The medics had a difficult time checking Frank's condition and finally decided to take their troop seats and strap in. Frank being fully secured inside the bubble with safety straps and tethered with hooks from the outside, the medics were confident that he would ride through the turbulence without any problems. With strong tailwinds it wasn't long before they were hovering over the landing site at Telluride Regional Medical Center. The bird was practically pushed all the way in. After a difficult landing, complements of down drafts, the medics and some of the mountain rescue team moved Frank to the ER vestibule and greeted the waiting ER team. After the hand off the medics stayed behind to brief the hospital ER while the mountain team went back to the helo to gather the team's gear.

Frank became lucid again and could see men and women around him talking quietly to one another. He looked around at the hallway with white walls surrounding him. *Where was he?* As he continued to take in the scene a stirring of familiarity came over him. The horror of it all struck him like a thief in the night. He remembered about his ordeal and that he was going to be air lifted to Telluride Medical Center. He must be at the hospital, but why are there hunters here with their gear and rifles? *How strange*, he thought. He didn't recall seeing them in the helicopter, but here they were and even though he had never met them he knew their names. But how could this be? Was it through his dreams or was he hallucinating? He looked up through the bubble and tried to get the attention of the medics. He had to tell them. The hunters' names were Jim Hazelton and Humberto Sanchez and they were in mortal danger somewhere on the mountain freezing to death.

But how could this be? Frank was seeing them standing right before him. He was either hallucinating or something or someone was causing this.

As he peered through the clear bubble again he could now see the hunters looking out in the distance at something. But what was it? How could they be in the hospital and on the mountain at the same time. Then an odd feeling came over him almost as if he was clairvoyant. How did he know about Hazelton and Humberto? Where did the thoughts come from? How did he know they were professional hunters? My God, could it be the wolf from his childhood dreams? Was there a connection between him, the hunters, the wolf and reality? Or maybe it was the good wolf from his childhood dreams and also the double-goer connecting with him. In essence, good versus evil. Joy, happiness and peacefulness versus resentfulness, anger and fear. He frantically banged against the inside of the bubble, but no one seemed to hear him. His imagination was now running rampant and he was afraid that he might be undergoing some kind of psychotic breakdown. He had to grab a hold of something, anything that would tether him to reality. Otherwise, he may never come back and be forever lost in the doldrums of time. *Where was Alice?* He questioned again. Oh yah, she is already here or so he was told. My God, is she really here? Frank frantically thought about his wife. He was confused and unsure of himself. He thought she was home in Wilmington, North Carolina. What was the wolf with astonishing blue eyes trying to tell him? Was he really connected with this wolf and he finally came full circle to realize that this all was happening and the wolf was his protector. He thought, *time has a way of catching up to your weaknesses and his could be psychosis?*

FORTY-THREE

Manifestations

T he sun rising over the majestic San Juan mountains cast its early morning glow on the Sheriff's office in Telluride. It was mid-April, and a beautiful morning was in store. The snow was just starting to melt and the exhilaration of something good was in the air. Captain Jason Whitfield could tell that it was going to be an early spring because some of the wildflowers on the mountain already started to bloom like the Glacier Lily and Wild Irish Blue Flag. He was still troubled about the circumstances surrounding Frank and Alice Thompson and the hunters. The Thompsons had left for Wilmington, North Carolina nearly two months ago, but the mystery didn't. In fact most of the law enforcement agencies in the area were still troubled by some of the events and were waiting for the thaw on the upper mountain to lie to rest all the stories and rumors floating around about the hunters. But that was only the tip of the iceberg.

Frank's health and medical condition improved greatly once he was admitted to the hospital. His extremities mainly recovered from the frostbite except for a little numbness in his toes.

Mentally though it was another matter, not for him but for his wife. Alice insisted there were five hunters on the mountain hunting big horn sheep. And she was right as far as that was concerned, but she also insisted that she was saved by the hunters when the cabin caught fire; that Alice was there. Physically, she was doing fine. The last he heard from them was that they were still in intensive counseling with a team of psychiatrists with lots of letters behind their names. *I would be too*, Jason thought.

He reached down to the lowest filing cabinet drawer on his desk and once again pulled out the file. There was no name on it and people just referred to it as the 'file'. It almost had a supernatural mystique to it. In all his years in law enforcement he couldn't ever recall coming across a case like this. It was the most fascinating story that he ever been involved in. And the mysteries in the 'file' keep evolving and will evolve for sometime. He was sure of it. As he thumbed through the thick folder, his thoughts turned back in time to all the unanswered questions.

Like the satellite phone call that Denise Roberts received at the 911 call center. Without that call the Thompsons' wouldn't have made it. *But who made the call?* Jason thought. Alice said that Jim Hazelton made the call after rescuing her from the burning cabin. Except it was the Guard that found and rescued Alice. And Denise claims that the call was a satellite 211 prefix without any call header or identification. Denise said that the voices that came through her headset were garbled and scratchy, but she made out the names Alice and Franco or Francis or possibly Frank and she was pretty sure that they were asking for help. *Was this divine intervention?* Jason thought.

To this day Alice swears that all five hunters were there at the cabin. She knew their names and what they looked like, even though she had never met or spoke to them before. *How could this be?* Jason thought. She also swears that Clyde Easton, Earl Garvey and Leroy Hazelton, Jim's son, were also on the life flight back to Telluride. Jim Hazelton and Humberto Sanchez hung back and didn't go because they wanted to find out more about the disappearing wolf tracks. The state and county sent out multiple search teams and they searched far and wide, but so far there was no discovery. They didn't even find any equipment that belonged to the hunters. It was if they all vanished from the face of the earth. He should know he conducted two of the searches.

Now here is where it really gets interesting. Alice never saw the wolf tracks that disappeared in the snow, but she claims the hunters did. Her husband, Frank claims that he had seen them on at least five occasions and described them in great detail right down to scar on the right fore pad. According to him the paw prints had a strange symmetry to them. The fore paws and hind paws were nearly perfect in shape, except for the scar, but the depth of the tracks didn't match the size of the prints. In other words they were much shallower than what they should be for a wolf of that size. Frank said the creature was huge at about 140- pounds. In addition to the disappearing tracks the creature was translucent with needle-like gray fur. Its sky blue eyes were piercing as if the creature could see right through you. As foreboding as the entity appeared, Frank claims that it actually was trying to help him find his way to Telluride, and if it wasn't for the creature he would have never gotten out of the crevasse. Jason shook his head thinking how incredible it sounded.

To make matters more bizarre, Frank also claimed that the phantom wolf had an evil twin–the same one that attacked him. A doppelgänger if you will. When asked how he knew this, he said that they were identical in size and shape, except the real wolf had deep blue eyes instead of sky blue eyes and wasn't translucent and didn't have needle-like fur. Of course everyone was stunned at this revelation.

Jason shook his head again thinking about the shrink reports that he had received in the past week. He was forwarded a copy for the investigation. He knew that working through the psychiatric reports was going to take some time and he would have to get professional help in this area. In particular one report did catch his eye. It had to do with dream therapy and hysteria. In the report, Dr. Schoenfield indicated that a person could gain insights to his dreams by remembering the various elements that compose his dreams or stories and interpret those in a logical manner in order to better understand himself. Also, a person could revisit other dreams that he had in the past and that he could come in anywhere in that dream, and this could happen multiple times over a period of time. He further deduced that a person not only could connect with his own dreams but also could connect to other peoples' dreams on a subconscious level. He entertained a theory that if you could connect to other people perhaps you can control and propagandized them. He theorized that this in part would enable a person to control another person through hysteria by using vehicles such as fear. And then the doctor blew the doors off. He conjectured that there might be a link between humankind and the animal kingdom on the subconscious level. And, if this is the case then humans may be able to control animals on the subconscious and primal level and animals might be able to control humans.

Dr. Schoenfield and his team tested and questioned Frank and Alice Thompson extensively along with their background and family history and came up with the unimaginable. They think since Frank had frequent and lucid dreams of a huge gray wolf as a child that somehow that same wolf manifested itself in Frank as in adult, especially under extreme stress. This enabled the real wolf to take control of Frank through his fears of failure. The other wolf-like creature represented the good in Frank and only wanted him to succeed. The age-old struggle of good vs. evil ensued and manifested itself in these two wolves through Frank's hysteria.

The doppelgänger was victorious against his evil brother in splitting good from evil and ensured that Frank would succeed this time. By doing so, Frank saved himself and his family and finally came to terms with his life.

EPILOGUE

Alice heard the alarm go off and waited a minute before turning it off. It was Saturday morning and Frank stirred besides her trying to gain consciousness. "Hon it's the weekend and why don't you stay in bed for awhile. I'll get up and fix us some coffee." Alice said. She got up, put on her pink slippers and bathrobe and ambled out to the kitchen. After getting the coffee going, she sat down at the kitchen table waiting for the Keurig Coffee Maker to finish when she suddenly spied her florescent orange hair band on the floor next to her leg. After picking it up she experienced the strangest feeling wondering why the hair band was here. If she didn't know any better she thought her hair band should have been found elsewhere, but where, she thought. Just then Frank came in to the kitchen smelling the aroma of coffee. "Morning, hon," he said looking in her direction. He looked into her blue eyes and could tell something was troubling her. "What is it, honey?" Frank asked. While waiting for an answer he shuffled over in his slippers to get some coffee. "Honey, did I ever have more than one florescent orange hair band?" She asked. "I don't know, hon. I'm sure my job, in addition to everything I do around here, doesn't involve keeping track of your hair bands. Wait a minute, how come this is so important to you?" He rubbed the stubble on his face waiting for an answer. Alice looked at her husband, deciding on how to answer this. "I could have sworn we were in our cabin in the middle of winter, running out of fuel or wood for heat and more importantly food, and you had to walk to Telluride to get help. The last thing you took before you started your trek was my florescent orange hair band for luck. I'm worried, dear." Alice muttered. Frank gave his wife a really hard steady look. "My God, you are really upset aren't you?" Frank exclaimed. "So you think this was a dream?" Frank asked. "Honey this was really more than a dream. It has shaken me to the core. "Frank, are we really home?" Alice asked. He ran a meaty hand through his course gray hair, trying to think what happened to his wife.